# KHASATI

A Novel by
## A Northern Female

**Instagram:** @anorthernfemale
**X:** dnorthernfemale
**Website:** www.anorthernfemale.com


**Designed & Publish:**
Emphaloz Publishing House
www.emphaloz.com
publish@emphaloz.com


ISBN: 978-0-307-34798-5

**Available Globally**

# Dedication

This book is dedicated to every Northern Nigerian female. Your dreams are valid, and as you walk your path, you will make them real.

# Introduction

The book *Khasati* contains words in the Hausa language from Northern Nigeria.

# Contents

# CHAPTER 1

Imagine what life would be like without pain. For me it would be when I was a lot younger, oblivious of so many things. Just a girl with pure childlike innocence. I find solace in those memories, especially in moments like this when life is giving me a bitter taste of existing.

A familiar feeling of happiness and calm comes over me whenever it rains in my hometown. It's the smell of the soil when the first drops hit the ground, that earthy scent does something to me. Sometimes, I even crave the taste of it. I find myself wanting to put a handful of that damp sand in my mouth. It has a beautiful, rustic smell. It's a weird feeling.

I used to sit outside on our veranda, watching the rain fall. Sometimes, I would stick my nose out the window just to feel the fresh air hit my face. There was this overwhelming feeling of bliss that I still can't explain. Other times, I would crawl under my blanket and lie still as the wind blew through the window, the cold air teasing my skin. It's a weather that brings an undeniable comfort, a feeling I crave now. I need it now.

It would do me a lot of good to feel an ease that starts from the surface and seeps deep into my soul enough to let me sleep for a while. I need it.

I am in so much pain that my mind is reaching for old memories and scenarios that once made me feel whole, back when I was much younger, a child, carefree, with no emotional baggage or regrets.

I usually know how to get my life back when life kicks me. It's the typical thing everyone does to elevate themselves the 'glow-up phase'. You channel your pain into taking care of yourself. You upgrade. You make your past self look like a stepping stone. But this time, I'm not sure I can do it. I want to, but I just can't pull myself together.

I'm awake, yet I don't feel like leaving my bed. I'm too broken, searching for ease but finding none. My heart feels heavy. I am drowning in this pain. I keep longing for nighttime, to curl up in the dark and beg sleep to take me. I hate daybreaks. The night is better even though it brings nightmares. When I close my eyes, I just toss and turn with tears lodged behind my eyelids. Morning always greets me with migraines and bloodshot eyes. I hate living like this.

My phone is on silent, and I don't like picking up my calls. When I do, I end it quickly. I need relief, but I'm not ready to look for it. It feels like nothing can help. Instead, I sit in my doom, hoping time will pass by quick, maybe then I can feel some ease. But sitting in this room feels like hell itself.

How can something so soothing turn into my worst nightmare? To call what I felt 'Love 'is an understatement, what I felt was more than love. It was sacrifice, Passion and Devotion. But all of it was spat on. I was shameless in my vulnerability. I let my guards down, and now I am paying for it.

I was told my standards were too high, that I should look at life with an open mind and just date for the simplicity of it. So, I tried. And I learned a valuable lesson: "**NA MIJI MAYE NE** '*men are witches*". They meet a happy girl and ruin her. No normal person treats a woman like this... unless, of course, he is a witch.

One thing I have learned is to never lower your standards for any man. Let them rise to your level. Date someone who understands your core values, principles, and way of life. You are not being difficult; it is simple math.

I know love comes with understanding and a fair share of compromise, but some things are non-negotiable. Your principles are non-negotiable. Stand on them. Insist on them. When you slack or accept anything outside of who you are, prepare for the worst. If he does it twice, he will not stop. You either leave, or you waste precious time and days that eventually turns into years hoping he changes. A man will only be "the one" if he is ready. Do not compromise.

I learned this lesson the hard way. And I am still paying for it.

This is more than heartbreak; this is heart-wrenching pain. It feels like my heart is a small, wet towel being squeezed until the last drop is forced out. I can't believe I am in this much pain. I would do anything to not feel this way. I hate him now, but I still wish I was in his arms. I want him to fix what he broke, to lie to me a little longer, to tell me everything will be okay. I need him here just a little while, because I can't handle this pain alone.

I hate this version of what I have become. I hate this state I am in. I am broken. I am deeply hurt. I would take anything that could speed up this phase and get me over it.

For someone who gives the best relationship advice, I make the worst decisions when choosing a partner. When the despicable traits began to show, I should have left. But I convinced myself it was all part of loving someone. The things I did for love are too shameful for the kind of woman I am. I will take them to the grave before I tell anyone the humiliations I endured. It is too shameful because it cannot be me of all people.

Hmmm.

I was foolish. Even thinking about it now, I collapse inside. I was foolish.

No one must ever hear that Hallittah was this stupid. How have the mighty fallen because of love? I used to not care about men... No emotions. Just a cold woman who loved the idea of love but never gave it a chance until this big mistake.

I loved a man. His named Jason.

He was my type tall, dark-skinned. We were great together. He hovered over me and made me feel cute. He felt like forever. He seemed like he had his life put together. He spoke so well. He knew so much politics, history. I admired him. If he didn't tell you otherwise, you would think he was well-travelled, but no he was just smart. He loved to learn and spent his time watching documentaries and podcasts on YouTube. I loved everything about him.

He provided solutions to my problems without me ever asking. He was the first person I called in the morning and the last person I spoke to before bed. I was the first person he would call to complain about his workers or when he had an altercation with someone. We were great until we were not.

I had taken so many "sorry", swallowed so many humiliations, that every other good thing he did began to feel useless. I was the one who ended the relationship, but it felt like he wanted me to by putting me through hell so I could make the first move. Why would you claim to care for someone and still hurt them?

I wanted to channel the pain as fuel to ignite my life, my career, anything that could upgrade me or distract me from this moment. If only I could make the first step. My mind was ready, but physically, I couldn't bring myself to even get up.

Before Jason, I was already dealing with the loss of the most important man in my life. I was sad, but I still took great care of myself. Caring for myself was instinctive, a habit ingrained from childhood.

As a Northern Nigerian girl, beauty rituals are part of our upbringing. From a young age, a girl is taught how to embrace her feminity, cleanliness, beauty tricks, herbs, and intimate care as she grows older. For most people, these practices are meant to prepare a girl for marriage, but for me, they became a lifestyle. With or without a man, it was my thing.

My friends teasingly called me *Mamalawo* 'female herbalist' because I had herbs for everything in my apartment and blends of oils for every part of the body. I never ran out of *humra*, a special mix of ointments and scents used as perfume by Northern women. I had different collections, and the beautiful thing about *humra* is that the older it gets, the richer the scent becomes.

I knew how to blend oils and butters for my skin. I knew how to make comfort teas during my menstrual cycle. I loved myself, and I extended that care to everyone in my life, male or female. On some weekends, I hosted my friends for girls' nights just us applying masks, muds, oils, drinking tea, and chit-chatting.

I was ambitious too, but lately I had become comfortable with earning just enough. Life took a sudden turn when I lost my dad. My momentum to push for more disappeared. I was deeply hurt. I was daddy's girl. I woke up one morning and he was gone. It hasn't even been a year, so I was taking things easy on myself. My routine became simple: work, gym, home. That pattern kept me grounded.

My phone buzzed again. Chiamaka was calling. She had called two days earlier, and I had responded with the automated text: "Busy, I will call you back." But I never did. I was about to switch off my phone when I heard a knock on my door.

I knew it was her. I didn't know how she managed to pass the security guards at the gate, as no one was allowed in without a code. But she always found her way.

"Open this door, I know you are inside!" she yelled.

I dragged myself to the door. She came in, dropped the bags of food she was carrying, and hugged me. I expected her usual lecture, but instead she brought love wrapped in silence. I melted in her arms and cried.

After a while, she opened the food she brought. Bread and suya a Nigerian delicacy of grilled meat with spices, with a big bottle of Coca-Cola my comfort food. Everyone who knows me knows I will never say no to suya and bread.

Jason and I ate this almost every weekend. We would park in front of my house or sit in the parking lot of the suya spot and eat together. It was our thing.

My mind was drifting again, forgetting that Chiamaka was right there. I smiled faintly and kept eating in silence. We didn't say a word to each other. She stocked my fridge with the remaining foodstuff she brought, cleaned up after we finished eating, then pulled me down beside her on the carpet, adjusting my head on her laps. The silence was needed, soft, and grounding until we eventually drifted into a nap.

When we woke up, I whispered, "Thank you."

"Just because i didn't say anything doesn't mean I won't drag your butt if you refuse to pick my calls," she said. "I know it's hard, but you gotta move on. Don't give Jason this much power over you."

She hugged me again before she left.

If I could, I would delete the day I met Jason.

I met him at the supermarket near my house. I was heading towards the exit after grabbing some essentials when he stopped me to compliment my head tie. I smiled and said thank you. He was the first man to ever tell me I looked beautiful wearing a scarf. In a world where men mostly praise wigs and extensions, it felt refreshing to be seen like that. I wear extensions sometimes, even a wig if I'm in the mood, but most days, I prefer to tie my head scarf with a little bit of my hair peeking out.

I walked to the farmers' market beside the supermarket to buy beetroot and fresh parsley for juice. I barely noticed someone standing close until I almost bumped into him. I apologized.

"Are you one of those healthy-living type of girls?" he asked. "Because it is written all over you."

That was when I really looked at him. "Maybe," I replied.

That was how we met.

Jason. Tall. Dark-skinned. Exactly my type. He had the look of someone who spent time in the gym, with broad shoulders, easy confidence and a clean-shaved beard that suited him too well. He walked beside me, talking effortlessly. I found myself interested almost immediately. He was detailed when he spoke, intentional, and he listened like he could see through me. Before we left the market, he asked for my number, and we exchanged contacts.

Four days later, he called. The moment I heard his "hello," I knew it was him, but I pretended not to. "It's Jason," he said. "We met at the supermarket some days back."

"Oh, hi Jason."

"I passed by the farmer's house in downtown Abuja today. They had fresh beetroots and parsley. It reminded me of you. I bought more than I need, and I thought I could drop some off for you if you don't mind. They're really fresh. I think you'll like them that is, if you don't mind," he repeated.

"I would love that."

"So, where do you live? I could drop by in 30 minutes."

I lived close to the supermarket just a street away, so it was easy for him to find. In 25 minutes, he arrived with an unbelievable amount of beetroots, parsley, carrots, and apples. When he opened his boot, I gasped. It was *plenty* so much that the security guards had to help carry everything to my apartment. It was sweet of him, and I appreciated the extra fruits.

"Are you busy?" he asked.

"Not really."

"Do you want to sit and talk?"

I agreed but suggested we sit at the seating area beside my apartment. It was a small garden; it had always been one of my favorite places to unwind in the evening.

"Thank you for bringing the entire farm to my house," I said.

He laughed. "Yeah, my bad." "It will last you a while, before you buy them again"

We talked mostly about fitness, my obsession with eating healthy, and my beauty rituals. The conversation was easy; it flowed naturally. We even discovered something small but cute we shared together; we both loved the color black. And he believed, like I did, that being fit doesn't mean you must boycott your favorite meals. It's all about balance. It worked for me, and he agreed.

"You know," he said, "most fitness enthusiasts forget that different body types react differently to different foods. Fitness rules apply generally, but individuals are different. Just like in medicine, where doctors give professional advice but will still listen to the patient when they express their concerns, sometimes a patient says, 'I know my body,' and they're right."

"Are you a doctor?" I asked.

"Yes, but not practicing," he replied. "I do other things, like managing the business side of medicine and fitness."

Jason had a company that set up gyms and supplied medical equipments and medicines to hospitals.

"Naima, can I take you out this weekend?". He asked.

"How did you know my name is Naima?" I blurted. "I remember telling you my name is Hallittah."

"Truecaller showed your name as Naima," he said with a small smile. "And I loved it. If you don't mind, I'd love to keep calling you that. Naima sounds different."

"My grandpa named me Naima after his crush when he was a young boy in Gombe. I'll tell you the story someday, it's interesting".

"Someday... hmm, I like the sound of someday. It means you enjoy my company enough to promise a someday," he said with a smile.

Most people call me Hallittah; only a few knew me as Naima.

"Can I rush this 'someday' and make it this weekend? Can I take you out?" he asked again.

"I would have loved to," I replied, "but this weekend marks one year since my dad passed. I'd rather stay indoors."

"I'm sorry about your father," he said.

I smiled. He asked how he died, but I changed the topic I wasn't about to get emotional in front of a stranger. Jason understood and didn't push further. His sensitivity and attentiveness were among the many things I admired about him.

When the weekend arrived, I told myself I wouldn't be sad. But from Friday night, a wave of grief swept over me. I crawled into bed and cried. Morning came, and I felt no better. It was the one-year mark since my father's death, and the pain hit afresh. I had spent days in denial, pretending it wasn't real, that my father was still alive. But now, reality set in my dad was truly gone.

# CHAPTER 2

**E**ventually, I forced myself out of bed and didn't realize it was already 1:00p.m. until my phone beeped. Jason had messaged: *"Can I call you?"*

I reluctantly replied.

"Hi, Naima,"

"Hello,"

"Is today the day?" he asked

"Yes" I answered

"Uh-uh,"

"I'm so sorry for your loss," he spoke gently. "I understand if you don't want to talk, but I feel I could cheer you up, even if it's just staying on the phone with you. If you don't mind."

He asked me about my fondest memories of my dad, and I found myself opening up. My father was different from others I had seen growing up. In the Northern part of Nigeria where I'm from, the stereotype of father daughter relationships often overshadows reality. But our love was real. My father and I shared a unique bond. He loves listening to me ramble about my dreams and never failed to tell me he was proud. My teenage years were beautiful, because he was always there, fully present.

Apart from reading, my dad loved drinking teas, lots of Nescafé. And when I say tea, I mean the Nigerian version, not the English kind made from just tea bags and hot water. Nigerian tea was rich: hot water, powdered milk, Nescafé or Lipton, sugar, and sometimes Milo. My dad loved Nescafé, he drank it almost every day, at any time. It was his favorite ritual.

"Let's recreate that memory," Jason said. "If you don't mind."

It sounded funny at first, but I agreed. Later, he arrived at my house carrying a boiling kettle, teacups, big jars of powdered milk, sugar, and Nescafé in a basket. I came downstairs, and my eyes fell on the cups they had *I love Dad* written on them.

"How did you get these?". I asked.

"They sell them in the supermarket," he replied.

"That's so sweet. Thank you." I tried to fight tears from falling.

I brought him up to my apartment, and we sat on the rug, sipping tea. What was supposed to be a sad day turned cheerful. Jason kept me company, and I didn't even notice the hours passing.

When I got up to prepare food, Jason insisted we eat out. So, we hopped into his car and drove to get suya. I loved mine with a little fat, lots of pepper, and onions. Jason preferred his Suya the same way. He bought fresh baked bread for us to eat with the Suya, a combination I love eating growing up in the North.

We returned to my apartment and sat outside, using the car bonnet as a table while enjoying our meal. It was the perfect comfort meal, made even better by Jason's company. For a moment, I forgot my grief, and, for the first time, I felt a soft warmth towards him.

When it was time to leave, he asked me out on a date.

"I'd like to hear the story of how the name Naima came to be," he said.

I couldn't say no. His kindness and thoughtfulness had already won me over, and I was curious to see where this connection could go.

Jason picked me up on Monday for lunch. As I had predicted, the restaurant was nearly empty as it was a Monday, however, weekday lunches often offered the best service, fewer distractions, and a calm ambiance. He gently took my hands as we sat down.

"Can you tell me the story?" he asked.

I laughed at his eagerness. "Okay, I'll tell you."

"When my grandpa was a boy in the village, some Fulani people moved to an area not far from their family farmland, across a shallow stream. My grandpa and his brothers often went there to fetch water. One day, he met a beautiful girl with long, curly hair and brown skin..."

He always said she had the most beautiful eyes in the world. My grandpa was captivated by her beauty. He always looked forward to going to the farm just to see her. Her name was Naima.

Her father bought some land from my grandpa's father, and the families became close. Soon, almost everyone knew they liked each other. She gave him a special name that only she called him. She was clever and knew how to roast corn. Sometimes, my grandpa and his brothers would go to her house to scout for corn and wait for her to roast it. She would give him fresh cow's milk. He would tell everyone that one day he would marry her.

Her father was very wealthy and owned many cows.

She gave my grandpa a small bracelet made of strong yet soft twigs and a pure silver hairpin. In Hausa, it's called *masila*, used by women to loosen hair. My grandpa even stole his mother's mirror and gave it to her. One day, she disappeared. Days passed, and he couldn't find her until he learned she had been betrothed at birth, and her husband had come to take her away. He cried for days and refused to eat. Everyone laughed at him because, back then, Fulani rarely married outside their tribe, let alone to someone speaking a minority language.

He never forgot Naima. To him, she was the greatest expression of love, a story he shared with everyone. So when I was born, my grandpa swore I resembled Naima, that I had her features. Although my official name given by my parents is Hallittah, the name my grandpa gave me stuck. Some people, especially from home, still call me Naima.

"Wow, what a beautiful story," Jason exclaimed. "I can see why your grandpa insisted on naming you Naima."

I smiled.

Our conversation was briefly interrupted when the waitress got Jason' order wrong. I watched how calmly he handled it. When he told her it was incorrect, she apologized, and he insisted it was okay he ate what she brought. I had been on dates with rude men, and you could always tell from the way a man treated the waitress or the driver. It was a reflection of their character. It was a relief to see how kind and considerate he was.

From small glances to easy conversation, dinner went smoothly. Jason dropped me at home, kissed my hands, and said he would one day love to see my hair. I teased him, saying, "I'm bald."

He laughed. "I doubt it, given why you're named Naima. And even if you were bald, it wouldn't matter."

I got down, smiling. He had planted a thoughtful seed in my mind, and I found myself liking it.

The next morning, I woke up excited to visit the new gym that had just opened near my house. After returning home, I showered, took a hot bath, and made myself a cup of turmeric, cinnamon, and black pepper tea. This was one of my many morning rituals that kept me healthy. I believed drinking something hot in the morning did wonders for the body, especially when it was infused with herbs.

As a woman obsessed with keeping my inner parts healthy, this ritual was sacred. After my tea, I dipped my face into a bowl of cold water, one of my secrets for flawless skin. My routine always began from the inside and moved outward.

When my phone buzzed, I guessed right it was Jason.

"What are you up to this morning?" he asked.

"I'm checking out the new gym across from my house, Go Fitness," I replied.

"What time are you heading there?"

"Just about to leave."

"Alright, I'll call you back in an hour or two," he said.

At the gym, the facilities impressed me as I stepped in. I registered and started working out. About thirty minutes in, I noticed someone standing beside me. I turned and there was Jason.

"Hi, pretty. What are you doing here?" he teased.

"Oh, this is one of the gyms we were setting up. That day I met you at the supermarket, I was running errands for this place," he explained.

He smiled. "I guess I'll start working out here now, just to make sure you're safe and to keep everyone away from you," he joked.

"What do you think of our facility?" he asked.

"Impressive. I've never been to a gym this sophisticated," I replied.

"Thank you. That's what we do. We bring the best."

After finishing my session, I met Jason at the reception. He was chatting with a staff member, when he saw me, he excused himself and held the door open for me.

"Let me drop you home," he offered.

"I actually need to pick up some items from the mall, about ten minutes away," I said.

"Perfect, I'll drive you there."

At the mall, I bought groceries, and Jason picked some too for himself. He insisted on paying for mine despite my protests. When he dropped me home, he carried most of the groceries inside. Then he held my hands and said,

"Naima, I would love to date you. I want us to be a thing."

I smiled, "Let's see how it goes."

He kissed my hand. "That must be a yes, then."

"It's a 'let's see how it goes,'" I said.

He laughed. "I'll take that as a yes."

From that day, we spoke every day, worked out together, and soon everyone said we looked good together. He introduced me to his sisters and his father. I remember the first day at his family home; his elder sister was visiting also.

"Meet Naima," Jason said. "You'll be seeing her often."

She smiled, but there was something in her expression that made me uneasy. At first, I thought it was just because she was meeting me for the first time, but I later found out.

Jason became my person the first one I'd call if I felt uncomfortable, the one I could share everything with. We talked about business, friends, and daily life. I knew all his whereabouts, and being with him felt like home.

He once told me about his former business partner, Eve. They'd been friends for seven years before she left, leaving him heartbroken, because she was his best friend. He said she had feelings for him, but he never reciprocated. His family loved her and hoped they'd end up together. I began to understand why his sister had given me that strange look, it must have been odd to see another woman with him that wasn't Eve.

I always believed a woman should trust a man when he says he feels nothing. Love cannot be forced. I blamed Eve for not taking "no" for an answer.

With Jason, I grew softer. He lit me up. I loved the provider in him, the listener in him. He gave everyone around him nicknames he called me "Bubbly," his friend Kate was "Cheeky," and Eve was "Squirrel." Kate later became his assistant, she had an impressive marketing idea. She became like a big sister, someone I could confide in.

Jason is good looking he attracted many women, but I didn't care. He was faithful, even telling me about the advances he received, and we'd laugh about it. He filled the emptiness I carried from losing my father. He was more than a lover, he was also a father figure. My friends always said I was closed off to love, but with Jason, I gave it a chance.

As a Christian, I had beliefs I held sacred. Sex was not an option. Jason respected that. We kissed, cuddled, even had sleepovers, but never crossed the line. He gave me no reason not to trust him.

But we struggled. He had a hard time admitting fault. Sometimes Kate would intervene, siding with me and helping him see reason. I loved him too much to let quarrels weigh us down, but things took a darker turn.

One day, after a heated argument at the gym, I stormed off. Kate comforted him, and they ended up kissing. I only found out later when Jason, in tears, confessed. I had never seen him cry like that.

"I was vulnerable," he said. "I'm sorry."

His tears felt genuine, but the betrayal stung from him, and from Kate, whom I had trusted. I left, determined to end things. But everything he had done for me made it hard to walk away. Eventually, I forgave him, though I was still hurt. Every quarrel reopened old wounds, and my trust eroded.

Later, I confronted Kate. She admitted they had kissed twice when they first met, before Jason and I were together. He never told me. I thought it was a one-time mistake. When I confronted him, he said, "That was before us. That's why I didn't mention it." His explanation made sense, but something still felt off. My trust was fractured.

I became hyper-aware his movements, his messages all seemed suspicious. On my birthday, he brought me a huge box of gifts, held my hands, and broke down in tears. He begged me to forgive him. For a moment, I believed we could fix us.

But it didn't last. I later discovered he was sleeping with his workers, Kate, and two other women. I felt shattered. How could someone so sincere appear so cruel? My life had been wrapped around him. How did he find time to see all these women when he updated me daily on his whereabouts?

I was broken. For others, moving on might have been easier. For me, it wasn't. I had never given so much of myself before. The most hurtful part was the women, the ones who had laughed with me, greeted me warmly, even hugged me yet were part of his betrayal. How had I missed it?

The memories hurt even more. Before all these painful events, there was a time I fell ill and was hospitalized, Jason coincidentally fell sick too. Despite his illness, he insisted on visiting me, ensuring I ate and rested. I saw love in his eyes. Genuine love. But behind those sacrifices was deceit.

Jason was a master manipulator. He cried, appeared truthful, but left out crucial details. I became a detective in my own relationship, a shadow of myself. His tears fooled me. I hardly saw men cry, and when this grown man knelt before me, with tears, I believed him. I eventually became his victim.

I hated him. I hated the pain and betrayal. I needed a fresh start, something anything to take it away.

After Chiamaka left my apartment that evening, I told myself it was time to get it together. Later, she texted, inviting me out to Norris Café, our favorite spot. I usually drank tea at home, but Norris had a special Arabian tea I could never replicate.

I didn't want to go, but I knew I had to push past the hurt. I replied, "Sure."

That night, I slept through the night for the first time in weeks. The next morning, I woke with a slight headache but didn't cancel. I picked a simple outfit with a matching head scarf. Pain had changed me; it was written all over my face. My eyes told a story I tried to hide.

I brushed my hair, fighting tears. I didn't want to appear sad in public. Almost changing my mind, I pushed through. I poured cold water into a bowl and dipped my face repeatedly, then applied a snail facial cream, recommended by Chiamaka.I couldn't remember the last time I did my beauty ritual.

I mixed sugar, coffee, and black soap to scrub my body, rinsing with water as hot as my skin could tolerate. I felt reborn. I spritzed humra bathing mist, letting its scent elevate my mood. I dipped my face in cold water again, staring at the mirror I looked revived.

I massaged shea butter and vanilla oil into my skin until it glowed. Blow-dried my hair, sealed it with more shea butter and vanilla, added a touch of lip gloss, and I was ready.

At Norris Café, Chiamaka, Stella, and David (Chiamaka's male bestie) looked surprised, when they saw me.

"I didn't think you'd make it. And before you say anything, we were just gossiping about you," Chiamaka teased.

I laughed, shoving her playfully as she hugged me.

"I want a hug too!" Stella said, wrapping her tiny hands around us.

David waved. "It's nice to see you again, Halli."

I smiled, feeling a flicker of joy.

# CHAPTER 3

For the first time in weeks, I laughed genuinely. Chiamaka's jokes made the afternoon light. At one point, David and Stella stepped out to buy candles nearby. Chiamaka held my hand.

"I'm glad you came out. Even though I caught you zoning out sometimes, but I totally understand. You've helped me through my breakup before letting me help you through yours." she said.

Tears welled upon my eyes. I forced them back, lifting my head.

The next day, I felt the urge to go out again. The pain remained, but I knew I needed to start taking the steps. I decided to make Norris Café my spot to hang out, just to be away from my room. Chiamaka joined me often, and those moments helped me breathe again.

I hadn't worked in a while; I longed for a change of environment. I needed a fresh start. Heartbreak had turned me into a depressed cow.

One evening, as Chiamaka and I sat at Norris Café, I heard a familiar voice call my name. My heart sank. I had feared this moment, yet I knew it would come. I couldn't tell if I yearned for it or dreaded it. My feelings were complicated.

I turned to the voice, masking panic with a casual smile.

"Hey, Jason. How are you?" I said, as though life was perfectly fine.

"It's been a while," he replied, reaching for a hug. I stayed seated, extending my hand for a brief shake.

"How are you?" I asked.

"Great. And you?"

"I'm good."

He glanced at Chiamaka, but her sharp expression made him immediately look back at me.

"Well... just saying hi."

"Thanks," I replied, praying my heartbeat wasn't audible.

For a fleeting moment, I saw a familiar sadness in his eyes. But instead of breaking me, it brought relief. I was in a better place now strong enough that his betrayal wouldn't crush me completely.

That night, I cried alone. Later, a text came from an unknown number; "It was nice seeing you again". I knew it was him. I didn't reply.

But I also knew I needed a change of space.

That same evening, I applied for a writing retreat and got an approval from the organizers in the United States. I needed a new environment. I also made a bold decision to move out of my apartment before traveling. I wanted a fresh start waiting for me when I returned.

For once, I was grateful for my valid U.S. visa. Holding a Nigerian passport often comes with disadvantages, especially if you love traveling. But thanks to my past work, Contracts, and philanthropy, I was fortunate.

I spent the week comparing conferences and retreats, searching for something aligned with my passions women's empowerment, business, anything that spoke to my soul. I stumbled upon a seven-day writing retreat and, without hesitation, I made a partial deposit.

I wanted more than seven days; I wanted a month in the U.S. to clear my head. When I saw an option to extend my stay, I took it. I checked my savings, carefully planning my trip, accommodation, and finances.

To cut costs, I reached out to an old schoolmate to stay temporarily. I would have loved a short-stay apartment alone, but I couldn't afford it. Over the next three weeks, I sold most of my belongings. Chiamaka and Stella bought some items, and a friend of Stella's bought my furniture.

"So, you want to run away and leave us?" Chiamaka teased as I packed my humidifier. I smiled, playfully shoving her. I didn't want to sell it was a gift from Jason but letting it go made things easier.

"Come with me to check out some houses in Wuse," I told them. "I saw a few good options."

Chiamaka drove us. Out of all the houses, only one caught my eye, it had a balcony and plenty of space, though it needed a little touch-up. I learned that the landlord, Mr. Emeka, liked to meet tenants personally, but he was not in the country.

I pleaded with the agent to convince him to close the deal before I traveled. He promised to try.

On the drive back, Chiamaka asked, "I hope you're not doing all this because of that boy, Jason?"

I rolled my eyes. "I just want a fresh start, that's all."

"See who's talking," I teased Chiamaka. "Remember what you did when you broke up with your ex?"

We burst out laughing. "I swear, I'll drive off this bridge if you keep laughing!" Chiamaka threatened.

"Omo, that bastard landed me in the hospital. "Aaron it will not be well with you!" she cursed, sending us into another fit of laughter.

"Chiamaka, I thought you were born again?" I teased. "Shouldn't you be wishing Aaron well?"

"Please, abeg!" she shot back, and we laughed even harder.

Despite the jokes, my mind was set, I needed a new beginning even if it strained my finances.

On the day of my trip, Chiamaka dropped me at the airport. Just as I was about to check in, I noticed a missed call from the agent. I called back, and he said Mr. Emeka the landlord wanted a video call.

After checking in, I called him. He picked up immediately. I introduced myself, explained I was leaving the country for a month, and asked if my friend could stand in for me, sign the rental agreement, and pay.

He asked about my tribe, my work, and my plans.

"You sound like a good girl. No worry. You can sign with our lawyer when you come back." he said in his Igbo-accented English.

Grateful, I called Chiamaka to handle the payment. Finally, that part was settled.

When I boarded the flight, emotions overwhelmed me. Everything I had carried in the last three years losing my dad, the heartbreak, the moments I almost lost myself rushed over me like a storm. I tried to hold back tears, but my eyes betrayed me.

As I buckled my seatbelt, I lowered my head and said out loud to myself,

"It's going to be okay. I will be okay."

Traveling within the United States felt like traveling from one continent to another. This writing retreat caught my attention because it was located in a town called Spokane in Washington State. The camp called Tarena is situated close to a hillside and has some natural springs and a waterfall. The images on the website sold the event to me.

I took a flight from Abuja on a long, winding journey first to Frankfurt, Germany. From there I connected to Washington, D.C., then to Denver in Colorado, before boarding my last flight to Pasco in Washington, exhausted but determined. When I first saw the routes, I had to take, I almost gave up, but I told myself I was about to embark on a transforming journey.

I comforted myself that it was worth the wait. The layover in Germany was six hours long and it almost drove me mad. At some point, I almost cried out of frustration. If I was honest, I just felt like the torture I was putting myself through was not worth it. I blamed my ex, and the thought of him made me even more pissed. As I tried to deviate my mind, I told myself, *we are not carrying Jason along on this trip; it is me, myself, and the beginning of something extraordinary.*

When I landed in Pasco, I went into the rest room to freshen up. After washing my face at the sink, I brought out my 100ml of coconut oil and swished it in my mouth, pulling out all the chocolates and food residue stuck in my mouth. For me, this trick works better than mouthwash, and it is extremely safe.

I arranged with the organizers at camp Tarena, and a driver was to pick me up at the airport, for a 2 hours and 30 minutes drive to Spokane. This service cost me an additional 200 dollars, but I didn't mind. After picking up my luggage from the baggage claim, I headed out, and Mr. Zuniga the driver was waiting with a placard with my name at exit 2 in the arrival's hallway. He collected my big check-in bag as I followed him to the parking lot. From his demeanour, he looked very reserved. I was happy it was going to be a quiet ride so I could get some sleep.

But I could not sleep. Instead, I kept looking at landscapes as we drove through small towns and farmlands.

"Is this your first time here?" he broke the silence.

"Yes, it is my first time in Washington."

"You will love it. Camp Tarena is beautiful, one of the most beautiful places in Spokane".

"Do you live in Spokane?" I asked.

"No, I stay in the Tri-Cities area."

"Where is that?"

"The Tri-Cities are made up of Pasco, Richland, and Kennewick. I stay in Richland, but I mostly do private services for Camp Tarena and other institutions that are not close to Pasco, and for tourists vacationing here."

"That is great," I responded.

"We will be pulling up to a restroom area in some minutes. They have vending machines, just in case you want a snack or need to use the restroom." Mr Zuniga said.

"Sure." I answered. I didn't want to use the restroom, but I could use some minutes to stretch my legs and move around. I got some Sour Patch and gummies, which cost about 4 dollars from a vending machine, and we continued the journey.

I was too tired, but I was very cautious. I didn't want to sleep. Maybe I was a little bit afraid, but I was certain that the camp would have vetted Mr. Zuniga. Still, I remained alert.

We soon drove to a gate, and behold, a beautiful landscape filled with cabins just as advertised on the website. It was exactly as I saw it. I got down, looking forward to my adventure.

I was greeted with a smile by the receptionist, who had 'Sarah' written on her name tag. I gave her my booking reference while Mr. Zuniga brought in my luggage. I thanked him, and he left. Sarah called another staff member who helped me to my room. I collected my meal schedules, and I was told to come back to the reception by 5:00p.m. for further details. I was so tired, I couldn't wait to shower and sleep.

I used the welcome brochure in my room to connect to the internet and call my mum. I told her I was going for a conference before I traveled, but I didn't tell her all the details because I didn't know how she would react if I told her I was spending so much money to go to a writing retreat. When I opened my laptop, as expected, she had tried calling me several times via Skype and left several messages. At the first ring, she picked up.

"Haba! Baby na 'my baby'. I was worried."

"I am fine. I just got to my hotel, and I want to shower and get some rest."

"Alright, take care of yourself."

"I will."

I dropped my laptop and rushed to the restroom. The water was soothing and hot enough for my skin to tolerate. The steam from the shower hovered over the bathroom like a cloud. I stepped out, cleaned my body, and went straight to bed, tucking myself into my blanket.

I woke up and realized I was 30 minutes late for orientation. I quickly wore a simple dress, wrapped my hair in my head tie, applied some almond oil and humra on my skin. As I walked to the reception, Sarah the receptionist looked at me.

"You look well-rested." She said

"And I am late," I responded

"It's alright. You might want to grab some dinner at the dining hall before it is closed for the night."

"Thank you, I will," I replied and headed straight to the kitchen area as I was already starving.

Two ladies at the dinning were already packing up, but they brought a takeaway paper plate and allowed me to pack as much food as possible, along with some fruits. They brought a paper bag for me so I could put it in, I thanked them and left.

I headed straight to the welcome orientation. Everyone was seated silent while a lady with dark black hair was addressing them. I walked in and everyone turned to look at me, which made me shrug a little bit. I hate attention.

"I'm glad you are joining us. You must be Hallittah. Hope you had a great flight."

I smiled. "Yes, I did."

"I am Erica. We have been communicating. Please, have a seat."

The orientation hall was so beautiful. It was made with wood and soft pillows. The hall looked nothing like the brochure, it looked marvelous. It really is a writer's den with lots of bookshelves filled with books. It smelled like paper, old books, and had an aura of a library. Above all, it felt like an embrace, to the literary world.

"So guys, I hope you have a great experience in each room you have scheduled, and also lots of free time to be creative" Erica continued

"Would you like to introduce yourself?" she asked

"Sure." I got up. "My name is Hallittah. I am a book lover, and this is my first time at a book retreat. I am looking forward to learning as much as I can."

"You are welcome, Hallittah," everyone chorused.

We were dismissed, and Erica walked up to me.

"Hi Hallittah, you didn't miss anything. If you need any help, let me know. I hope you find your way around and enjoy yourself."

"Thanks, Erica."

Everyone was looking around, but I wanted to go back to my room, eat, and sleep some more, so I don't wake up late again.

I was pumped for the retreat. I was looking forward to the experience. I thought I was going to sleep easily but couldn't. I opened my luggage and brought out the shirt Jason gave me. I took off my nightwear and wore it. It still had a faint scent of him. I know I said we are forgetting Jason, but I brought a part of him with me to the very place I was going to seek a break and find some peace. Like a pill the t-shirt worked I slept off.

My alarm woke me up by 6:00a.m, even though the first class was to begin by 9:00a.m. I woke up, brushed, showered, scrubbed my skin with my sugar and coffee scrub, and washed up with black soap. I dried my body and smeared shea butter and some humra.

After a quick breakfast, I headed straight to the orientation hall, where we met Serena Guevera, a bestselling author, writer, and poet, who spoke about connecting emotions to our writing as the basis of writing. She made us understand how poetry sometimes is a spilling of emotions, and that we could use that also in many forms of writing.

What I thought was just going to be lessons turned out to be more than that, everything was beautifully taught. Serena told us that she started writing at age 29, after a bad divorce. What started as a journal of her thoughts to help her heal became a bestselling poetry. I learned so much, and we were given an assignment to meet in the evening. We were each asked to spend the remaining hours finding something and writing about it, we were asked to connect our emotions to our write and be vulnerable while at it.

# CHAPTER

After Serena's session, we had lunch and then spent the afternoon exploring the grounds. The retreat center was tucked into the woods, with winding paths, and small cabins scattered around. I found a quiet bench by a stream, sat down, and let my mind wander. The sound of water and the smell of pine trees were soothing. I pulled out my notebook and began to write, letting my emotions flow onto the pages. I felt free like the world outside didn't exist.

By evening, we gathered again for our writing assignment review. Each participant shared what they had written, and Serena gave feedback. I shared a piece I had written about longing and loss, carefully weaving in the emotions I had felt from the separation with Jason. I felt vulnerable, but also strangely relieved. Serena smiled warmly at me.

"Hallittah, you have a natural way of channelling raw emotion into your words. Keep nurturing this gift," she said.

Her words stayed with me long after the session ended. Back in my cabin, I opened my bag and took out the shirt Jason had given me. I held it to my face and inhaled his faint scent. It made my chest tighten, a bittersweet ache that reminded me of him. I closed my eyes, letting the memory wash over me.

The next morning, I woke early again. I had grown used to the rhythm of the retreat: early mornings, long walks, quiet moments, and focused writing sessions. Today's session was about character development and creating believable dialogues. The instructor, a novelist named Jonathan, emphasized the importance of observing people and listening to the subtleties of human interaction.

During a break, I wandered off to a small garden behind the main hall. A gentle breeze rustled the leaves, and I felt a sense of calm. I thought about my life back home. For a moment, I allowed myself to imagine a future where all my dreams aligned, where I could balance passion, work, and love life without the constant tension of loss and responsibility.

By late afternoon, we gathered again to share our character sketches. Listening to others' stories and creations was inspiring. I realized that this retreat was not just about writing it was about rediscovering parts of myself that I had neglected.

After the evening session, I returned to my cabin to eat the food I kept earlier for dinner. I ate quietly, enjoying the simple pleasure of being alone yet surrounded by beauty.

That night, I lay in bed and reflected on the past few days. I had begun to confront some feelings I had buried, such as grief, longing, hope, and anticipation. I knew the journey ahead would not be easy, but I also knew that this retreat was helping me build resilience.

The next few days followed a similar pattern session with authors, independent writing time, walks in nature, and evenings of reflection. Each day, I felt a little lighter, a little more attuned to my emotions and my writing. The connection between life and art became clearer, and I began to understand how my experiences could fuel my creativity.

On the fifth day, we had a workshop on dialogue and pacing. The instructor encouraged us to write a short story in a single sitting. I chose to write about the t-shirt of comfort a story of a woman navigating the complexities of love and loss drawing from my own experiences with Jason, and my attachment to his t-shirt and the hope for moving on. When I finished, I read it aloud to the group. There was a moment of silence, followed by applause. I felt proud, not just for completing the task, but for allowing myself to be truly seen.

By the end of the retreat, I had not only improved my writing skills but had also rediscovered a part of myself that had been dormant. The quiet moments by the stream, the feedback from instructors, and the shared experiences with other participants had given me clarity.

The retreat ended, and I had a whole week to myself. I spent it writing and journaling, and slowly, my thoughts began to make sense on pages. My days were a mix of taking pictures outside and wandering through the local libraries and antique shops near Camp Tarena. It was an up-and-down week; some days were great, others I was overcome with sadness at night.

I realised I needed to make a firm choice to heal. So, I made the biggest move I could. I threw away my favourite t-shirt; the one Jason gave me. Parting with it was incredibly difficult, but I was ready. And the moment I did, I felt a wave of relief. I felt great. It was truly time to move on, and for the first time, I had no doubt.

After my time at Camp Tarena, I was already pumped to go home. I left Spokane feeling renewed, with a notebook full of new ideas, a heart a little lighter, and a mind ready to embrace the next chapter of my life.

I spent a week in Washington, D.C., with Temi, a friend of mine from university days. She was a business developer like me, and I wanted to catch up.

During the days we had together, I learned so much. She also connected me with some gigs back at home and introduced me to people she worked with in Nigeria. Overall, it was a productive week. I was ready to go back to Nigeria, get back on track with work, bid for some contracts, and schedule my life properly. I got the awakening I needed, and I was ready to work. Above all, I needed the cash.

After my three-week stay in the U.S., I headed to Washington Dulles Airport and boarded a Lufthansa flight to Frankfurt, Germany.

I met Zainab at the airport in Frankfurt, Germany, on my way back to Nigeria. She overheard me speaking Hausa to my mum and struck up a conversation. Zainab reminded me of myself a trait many Northern girls share calm and sweet. After a four-hour layover, we boarded the Lufthansa flight. I usually hate layovers, but with Zainab, time flew. By chance, the seat next to her was empty, so I settled in beside her.

When we landed in Abuja, she insisted on dropping me off at my hotel instead of letting me take an airport taxi. Before we got into the car, I noticed someone waiting. Everything about him screamed *well-mannered*.

*"Hi, you must be Hallittah,"* he said. *"Zainab told us to expect you."*

*"That was quick, nice to meet you,"* I replied.

He nodded politely, then helped the driver load our luggage. I'm not exaggerating when I say no light-skinned guy had ever stopped me in my tracks, but Saleem did. He spoke with poise, his Hausa accent peeking through his polished English. I had to remind myself to snap out of it. *It would be rude to meet someone's brother and immediately start dreaming of "happily ever after."*

During the ride to my hotel, Saleem and Zainab bantered about why she should leave the U.S. and move to London with him. They playfully argued over which city was more reckless. Their sibling dynamic was endearing.

*"Hallittah, I told you my Yaya (elder brother in Hausa) is getting married. You should come if you're still in town,"* Zainab said.

*"I'll be around, but none of my outfits are Arewa-wedding worthy,"* I laughed. *"I don't have anything fancy or modest enough."*

Zainab insisted anything would be fine, but I shook my head.

*"I know my Northern people it's not fine."*

We both laughed.

They dropped me off at my hotel, and we exchanged contacts. The next day, Zainab called, and we made plans to hang out. Saleem came along.

*"Hi, Hallittah,"* he waved. I smiled back.

*"He's our driver for the day,"* Zainab announced. *"Only way my parents let me move around this town alone. Either the family driver chauffeurs me around, or Saleem has to come."*

Saleem cut in, *"She chose me because she enjoys making me suffer."* He pinched her ear, and she swatted at him playfully.

*"By the way, Hallittah, let's go to my fitting,"* Zainab said. *"I think I have extra fabric left. Nuru can whip something up for you to wear to the wedding."*

We sat in the back, chatting and laughing while Saleem played an Amherdy song, a famous northern Nigerian musician. Zainab leaned forward to turn up the volume, and we all sang along. It was surreal meeting someone and instantly feeling at home.

After my measurements were taken, we drove to their house in Old Maitama. Saleem helped carry some of the *aligogoro* (head ties) we'd picked up from a vendor in Wuse. As we walked inside, I spotted a book by Rumi on the counter. My gaze lingered I *desperately* wanted to flip through it (*it's Rumi, for God's sake!*), but I held back, not wanting to seem rude.

Later, while relaxing in Zainab's room, Saleem walked in holding the book.

*"Is this how to bait you?"* he asked, a smirk playing on his lips as he gestured to the book.

I grinned with delight

*"You know Rumi?"* he asked

*"I breathe Rumi,"*

He laughed, and Zainab groaned. *"Ugh, please don't start with the poetry and prose thing.*

*By the way, Saleem has a whole collection of this old man's work."*

My eyes lit up.

*"Hallittah writes,"* Zainab told Saleem.

*"Interesting,"* he said, placing the book near me before leaving.

After what felt like forever greeting nearly every member of Zainab's family it was time for me to leave. Saleem reappeared, another book in hand.

*"This one's for you,"* he said, handing it over. *"It's by a scholar who studied Rumi's work. One of my favourites."*

Butterflies erupted in my stomach. *The way to a writer's heart? A book about her favourite poet.*

When I opened the first page, I found a handwritten note from Saleem:

*"When you read Rumi, breathe for two, because this would steal it away. A good book is like a memory you won't forget easily "I hope this is one."*

Signed with an **S.**

My fingers lingered on the page, tracing the words again and again. *This is how you catch a soul like mine* - simple words holding deep meaning. The first chapter pulled me under its spell. I didn't even notice when we arrived at my hotel.

Ahmed, the driver, dropped me off. Zainab couldn't see me off - her *lelle* (henna) was still drying on her palms. "Stay for dinner," she'd begged, "so it doesn't smudge before I see you off." But I had to rush back - a job contract bid needed submitting.

In my room, I devoured Saleem's book, page after delicious page, until my phone buzzed past 10:00PM.

"I'd bet anything you're still reading."

No need to guess who. I snapped a picture of the book covering my face and sent it.

"Hmm. Same clothes from earlier? Couldn't wait, could you?"

I grinned, feet wiggling like an excited rabbit, and replied with a blushing emoji.

"Hallittah, go to bed," he wrote. "Give those eyes a break - from screens and books. (P.S. I stole your number from Zainab's phone.)"

"Ok."

My coconut head obeyed without argument. Shower. Snacks. Sleep.

Morning came with Zainab's text - a photo of her finished *lelle*. I sent back a heart emoji; *love it* I replied.

"Today is *Kawyawa*! You must come!"

*Kawyawa* meant transforming into a Hausa villager. The girls wore mismatched Ankara wrappers, black *eye pencil* lining on our lips and forehead dots. The boys played Fulani herders, some stuffing shirts like *gwaza show* clowns, stumbling in oversized grandpa shoes.

Music pulsed. Laughter and spice hung thick. I piled my plate high with *awara* (tofu) and pepper, pretending not to scan the crowd for Saleem.

Then - a voice behind me.

"Hi."

I turned. "Been here awhile," he said, grinning. "Watching you attack that plate. With that much *awara*, you'll befriend the toilet tonight."

He stole a bite, then Zainab's chair, plopping beside me. She yanked at him, but he held her off with one arm. The sight of her struggling in her *Kawyawa* outfit made me laughed hard, and the pepper from the awara choked me.

Saleem lunged for water and passed it to me.

"Your fault!" Zainab scolded as I gulped, tears streaming from pepper and laughter.

"Are you okay?" Saleem asked, brow furrowed.

I nodded, still coughing.

Zainab left to get us *fura* (millet and fermented milk). Saleem's gaze stayed worried. "Sit up," he murmured, "so you feel better." He looked worried.

She brought two bowls of fura and left to meet her cousins, "Saleem keep Hallittah company I am coming." she said as she walked away

Saleem asked if we could take a walk, we strolled around the compound, as he explained the Hausa empires that existed before the Fulani's. He spoke of Hausa poetry, and authors who were renowned for writing great love stories. Listening to him had me fighting the butterflies in my tummy. He spoke of Turkey, of libraries holding Rumi's original Persian scripts. Poetry. Books. His humour was sweet, our rhythm easy.

By nightfall, Zainab strong-armed me into staying. As we scrubbed off her makeup, she smirked. "My brother *never* comes to these things. He Has his own place, but he sleeps here since I returned. Thought it was for me...but it's *you*."

I waved her off. "Nonsense "

"He lost his fiancée two years back," she interrupted. "Seeing him care again? It matters."

*That* explained his panic when I choked - love leaves ghosts in the living. I know a trauma response when I see one, it exaggerates danger.

Saleem, and his cousins Ibrahim, Aisha and Halima joined for a movie. We burrowed under blankets, sharing popcorn. Saleem sat close; I caught his glances, which were direct yet soft.

We dozed off after watching, waking up to the sound of the morning prayer call.

# CHAPTER 5

L ater that day we drove out for pancakes and hot chocolate.

"Thank God Zainab didn't snore like a hippo," Saleem teased.

"Wayoooo! Lies!" You cow I don't snore.

I was laughing at their banters

His text buzzed: "Love your smile. (P.S. Food in your teeth.)"

I panicked, checking

"Got you."

Saleem started talking about another poet from Morocco.

Zainab groaned. "Not poetry again!"

We drove to Nuru and collected my dress for the wedding and thereafter, I spent the night at Zainab's.

We all got ready in the morning and joined the convoy to the wedding.

The wedding was Northern opulence - gold-draped guests, fashion fit for emirs. Saleem sat close. "You look gorgeous, *Hallittan Allah*," he said, dropping the *H* from my name, and adding an N which translates to 'Gods creation'

Between admiring outfits, I texted my carpenter frustrated, trying to explain the wood needed for my apartment that I paid for before traveling, Saleem snatched my phone. "Let me," he said, rattling off measurements in fluent Hausa with the carpenter.

Saleem offered to drop me off, I knew he had asked Zainab. Zainab walks in few minutes later and suggests that Saleem drops me off and that I come back later, as though it was her decision.

Zainab's terrible acting did not fool me. At my hotel, I changed, while he waited in the car then he suggested we toured my empty apartment.

"Sofa here," I said, pointing. "Books there.

We toured every part of the apartment.

Next day, a truck arrived - filled with everything I'd described, that my carpenter was not making. "*My contribution*," Saleem texted. "*Hotels bleed money. I hurried things.*"

"*You didn't have to*"

"*I wanted to.*"

When he arrived later that same day, he brought out a handmade flour vase from a box in his car trunk, "you will need this more."

By weekend, I moved into my apartment. And I always had flower in my vase courtesy of Saleem. In no time my apartment felt cozy.

Zainab claimed a prayer corner in my living room, Saleem left Rumi books on my nightstand.

One balcony evening, while we wait for Zainab to be done praying, he turned to me, "Hallittah, you have my heart."

"The feeling is mutual I responded"

This love was slow, intimate without touch. He'd never held my hand, yet every note, every little gesture, every glance, every gift, felt like a warm embrace.

"I crave your presence," he said, voice soft.

"This must be what Rumi meant, 'the *earth has never known such feeling.*"

He drew his chair closer

*"Let me take you out on a dinner date."*

Zainab was peeping, he noticed *"you are not invited,"* Saleem teased.

*"Hmmmm,"* Zainab reacted.

*"God will judge you, Saleem. 'Kai kaman kulikuli' (head like kulikuli)."* We all laughed.

She left us.

His gaze shifted, staring deep into my soul. I couldn't look at him as I was shy. I bowed my head, unable to meet his eyes again.

*"You know what they say good people attract good people. You are easy to love Hallittah. Zainab hardly makes friends, but because of the way she is around you, I know you are no ordinary person. No Rumi lover is ordinary,"* he teased.

The following day, Saleem and I spent the evening at Moeshen Cafe at Life Camp Axis. We later opted to sit outside, to enjoy the captivating mountain view. The meals and mocktails really hit the spot.

Nothing hits deeper like a thoughtful man who knows what you like and drowns you in it. Every gesture feels like a testament to how much he cares. We later toured the art gallery on the 3rd floor, then came back upstairs. It was jazz night that Friday evening. Music was playing, but we were so distracted. A lot of eye contacts, smiles, small talks, and lots of teasing. He teased me with words; my soul was full. I could write a whole book about it. Maybe I should. In a short time, it feels like my whole existence does not compare to this short moment with this man.

The following weeks were filled with dinners at Saleem's family house and sometimes at his apartment. Zainab always came along.

When it was time for Zainab to travel back to the United States, my heart broke. I saw her off to the airport and cried a little. We held each other for what seemed like forever.

*"You goat,"* she pinched Saleem. *"Take care of my Hallittah. I will see you guys in 2 months. I need to be done with these exams."*

Towards the last weeks, I learned Zainab was rounding up her PhD at Columbia University in New York. Northern girls get stereotyped a lot, but yes, she is single, educated and smart just like many young Northern Nigerian girls.

The ride back home was quiet. Saleem didn't come up to my apartment as he is a complete gentleman. I know he only comes up when Zainab is around or when someone else is.

The only time Saleem came up to my room was when I was sick. Even though I insisted on self-medicating, he insisted I run a general test at the hospital to make sure I wasn't treating the wrong illness. He laid on the prayer mat Zainab left in my room while I slept off. By the time I woke up, he was already up, sitting on the chair next to me, excusing me to brush and freshen up for some tea. We went out for pancakes.

"Hallittah, I will be going to London briefly, but I don't want this to end. There's something I want to talk about, I know you have thought of it also; what our future would look like. I love you. I can't help it. I want you. I want to wake next to you. It takes a lot of self-control not to hold you. It hurts. And when you sit, your woody 'Humra' teases my senses, it makes me whole. You are my type, we have a special vibe. But I know what is in your heart. I know the questions."

Tears filled my eyes, and I noticed Saleem trying hard not to tear up. I didn't know how we got here from just enjoying each other's company.

Saleem and I are perfect for each other. He respects me. I know his family loves me from the extra souvenirs that Hajiya (their mum) gave me, to how welcoming everyone is. It felt great. We would make a great couple.

However, I come from a devoted Christian family; my father was a pastor and my mother, a deaconess. Even though I was born in the North, a Northerner through and through, I have always known religion to be the core and foundation of our existence.

Saleem interrupted my thoughts.

"Hallittah, can we navigate this big issue? I know we both have thought about it, but we've never addressed the elephant in the room. Can we navigate our religious differences? I want you. I want to spend the rest of my life with you. Can we take this to the next level?"

"I love you, Hallittah."

I was unable to control my tears. He reached out with a handkerchief to wipe my tears, making me shiver and cry more.

We drove back home. He handed over a handwritten note filled with deep expressions of love in Hausa and English, all dedicated to me. He handed it to me, walked me to my door. *"I will call you later."*

Alone in my room, I read, smiling and crying. This line struck me:

"Zuciyanki ba naki kade ba" (Your heart is not yours alone). "Apart from the path that is dedicated to God, give this man a chance, 'domin soyaya na (because my love) has been sieved in all honesty."

I texted him: *"Can we meet?"*

When he came, I joined him in the car, tears streaming down my face. "When we have kids, I know you are a devoted Muslim, and you would want them raised with that belief. I, on the other hand, would want to tell stories about David and Goliath, teach them cute memory verses, and bond with them. Won't you want your kids to be devoted Muslims?"

He said, "Yes. I want children." Then interrupted, "But we can decide not to have kids if that would help. We can be two selfish adults loving on each other you do your thing, and I do mine." I smiled at his seriousness.

"Love is beautiful, but it is not everything. Tomorrow, we might grow to want more than our young heart's desire, and the outcomes will destroy this love of ours," I said.

"I don't want to let this go."

"Me neither," I said. "But for how long?"

"You showed me love in a way I have never felt. You were loving me in ways words can't explain."

"Now I know how this love story would be like." He smiled, his eyes red. "What would you call this story of ours?"

"I don't know yet," I replied. "But You would be the first person to read it, if I put it into pages"

"Is this goodbye, Hallittah?" he asked I started crying. "No, it can't be, say something". I could only answer with my tears.

You would think Saleem is jobless, but he is a Software developer with a master's in data security. He is an analyst, an expatriate living in the UK. He works remotely in Abuja, when he is in Nigeria. He extended his stay in Abuja for me. He was due to go back to the U.K.

After what seemed to be the longest silence, we said our goodbyes.

I spent the evening, head hurting, eyes red-hot. I cried I don't want to let go. However, the thought of giving my mum a heart attack about marrying someone outside my religion, was splitting my head into pieces.

Half asleep, I woke up to a text by 5:00AM: "Can I see you?"

Saleem texted. Without hesitation, "Yes, please," I responded.

He came to my door with some books. He kissed me on the forehead for the first time since we met, his lips cold, tears rolling down my eyes. I noticed a teardrop from his eyes.

"I want to read this story of ours, when you are done writing it." Handing me more books, he smiled. "I am leaving for London; my flight is by 8 AM. Take care of yourself."

I felt weak. "Okay, stop crying..." He pinched my ear.

My legs froze. I went in, cried and cried. When I opened the first page of the book with the ribbon, it said:

"It begins with Rumi. Let us continue with Rumi, and maybe someday, we would find a love that has no ending etched in our souls. You will always have my heart."

Signed with an "S."

I spent the evening crying, I dragged myself to take some painkillers, took my pen and laptop, and I began writing.

Along the line, I lost the inspiration to continue writing and decided to drown myself in work. In the last few months, Chiamaka and I barely saw each other as we were both busy. She met Saleem once and gushed over how good-looking he was, but like everyone else, she knew how bent I was on not marrying outside my religion. Later, I received a text message from her that read, *"Take it easy on your heart."* I knew what she meant.

When Saleem left, it felt like a part of me was missing. I kept staring at my phone, waiting for a message, an email or anything at all. My spirit felt broken. So, I decided to call Zainab.

At the first dial, she picked up. "I was going to call you," she said. "Saleem calls every other day to ask about you. I felt something was wrong, but I wanted to finish my exams before reaching out. I even suggested he calls you, but he said you might want a break. Hope he didn't do anything to you, because I'll break his head."

I laughed. "I have missed you." She sighed.

"I miss you too".

"Sorry if I'm dragging this conversation, but you guys had something great going. I was so jealous. I'm too logical for love, and you guys seemed to do it so well."

"I know, Z," I replied softly. "I love Saleem so much, but we'll end up hurt. We can't marry each other. I can't marry anyone who isn't Christian. It may not seem like a problem now, but it will be in the future."

"My bad. I almost forgot you're Christian. Everything looked so perfect that I didn't pay attention to the religious differences."

Then she teased, "At least you can't marry me, so we'll still be friends." I laughed, but beneath my laughter was a sadness I couldn't hide.

"How is he?" I asked. "He's fine, but I know he's doing just as horribly as you. I know my brother too well. I'll call you again once I'm done with my thesis this weekend. Take care of yourself."

"You too," I whispered.

It comforted me that he was still checking up on me through Zainab, but deep down, I longed to hear from him directly. I had loved before, but this love felt unbelievable. Even though we weren't talking, it still felt like we were in a relationship. I was loyal even in his absence. Calling him would take nothing from me, but holding on to something with no future felt like self-sabotage. I loved this man, but I had to choose reason.

Just as I was about to sleep, a message dropped on my phone: *"I hope you are okay. I couldn't help but check up on you."*

I immediately called him. "Hey." "Hi." He let out a soft laugh, I felt it through the phone.

"I miss you," I blurted.

"The past days have been torture." "I miss you a lot," he replied. "You're making a grown man lose it. I stayed by my phone waiting for a message, fighting the urge to call."

"I thought I was the only one who felt that way," I said.

"Can we at least talk, even if we're not dating?" I asked.

"I would have suggested the same," he said warmly. "Now tell me everything. What have you been doing since I left?"

"Writing."

"Our book?"

"Yeah, but I lost my motivation."

"Writer's block," he teased.

"What about you?" "I've been messed up too. I try to catch up with work, but even with the flexibility, I've been miserable."

We spent the night on the phone, yet I didn't want the call to end. He had become my familiar place. But after a long silence, I finally ended the call. That conversation with Saleem was the energiser I needed for the days ahead.

# CHAPTER 6

C hiamaka got a job with a company in Victoria Island, Lagos, and was preparing to relocate. We began spending more time together. One evening at our regular spot, while we were chatting, Saleem sent me a picture of a beautiful view from his walk. A smile lit my face, and I quickly sent him a photo of my chicken Caesar salad and hibiscus drink. He replied, *"I guess you're with Chiamaka."*

"Yep." I took a quick photo of her trying to hide her face and sent it to him.

I dropped my phone, and Chiamaka gave me a concerned look. "What is it?" I asked.

"You look happy. I'm happy for you, but at the same time, I don't want you hurt. And before you get defensive, I know you're in love. I don't want to hurt your feelings as though I am policing you, but please, be careful."

I understood her, but I still clung to the hope that we could just be friends.

That night, I got on my knees and said a prayed. I asked God to take away the love I felt for Saleem and bring me someone meant for me because, I didn't want to be alone.

When I met Temi in the United States, she connected me with some Korean investors, who were setting up restaurants in 3 states in Nigeria, Abuja, Lagos, and Port Harcourt, covering the North Central, Southwest and South-South region of the Country respectively.

They consulted me on creating a strong marketing strategy. It was good money, and though I had no expertise in restaurants, I had ideas. I suggested merging Nigerian experience with Korean culture to create something new. I got the contract, to do the setup.

One evening, after my long skincare ritual, I was about to hop on a call with Saleem when Zainab rang. "Hey Hal, wallahi, I need your advice." "I'm all ears." She hesitated, then said, "You know I'm not all lovey-dovey like you. I don't even know what category of lover I am. But... I met someone months back before I traveled. He's Nigerian, based in Dubai and Abuja, from the Mai Riga family."

"You mean the famous Mai Riga?"

"Yes. My aunt introduced us. He's cool, responsible, and he's asked me to marry him. I like him, but I don't know how to place my feelings. How am I supposed to know if this is it?"

I listened quietly. Zainab was never one to talk about marriage. She was finishing her PhD and had always said most marriages were the graveyards of women's careers. But here she was.

"How do you feel about his proposal?" I asked. "Excited, but I still have reservations. I don't know what I'm supposed to feel outside of the short excitement."

"Do you like him enough to marry him?" I asked

"Definitely." She answered.

"Have you talked deeply about expectations; yours and his?"

"Well, he knows I want to be a professor and use my PhD. I want a family, but I also want to work in an Ivy League college. I assume he knows my stand."

"Don't assume, Z. Ask him. Put everything on the table. Then you'll know if it's the path you want to take."

"You're right," she admitted. "I'll do that. Anyway, I took a lecturing assistant job for four months to get experience. Once I wrap up, maybe I'll come back and see your face."

"Okay, silly," I teased. We both laughed.

By the end of the call, she was back to asking me for shea butter and *humra,* reminding me I'd make a fortune if I turned my body care products into a business.

Just then, my phone beeped again it was Saleem.

Weeks turned into months. Our bond deepened. Even though we called it friendship, beneath it was something more.

One evening, Zainab asked me to pick up perfumes for her, so I could ship it to the United States to her, worried about sending them through a dispatch rider. I didn't mind. When I arrived, my jaw dropped. Saleem was standing there, he was smiling, it felt like the ground trembled beneath me.

"Hi, Hallittah."

I froze, torn between hugging him and just staring. He stepped closer, kissed me gently on the forehead, and held my hands. I wanted to melt in his arms, but I held back I knew how cautious he was about touch. I could feel how much it took for him to do that, and tears threatened to escape my eyes.

We sat by the couch at the entrance of what looked like a spa, shelves lined with perfumes. "I just came into town. I didn't want you to suspect, I thought we could meet at a café instead, but I didn't want you to have a clue that we were up to something, he paused and took a deep breath, "I missed you," he said, it was written all over his eyes, I missed him a whole lot, the moment felt to real, I felt the excitement building inside my tummy. I smiled trying to ease whatever is going inside. I was so happy and even though I was not saying much, I knew he could tell.

I was still recovering from the shock when I remembered the taxi waiting outside. I quickly went and paid him extra and dismissed the driver, Saleem drove me to check out the Korean restaurant project.

The car ride was quiet, filled with awkward silence, though my insides danced with joy. "You smell like you, soft and calming," he said, breaking the silence. I smiled shyly.

"Well, you got me. This was one heck of a surprise."

After inspecting the restaurant, we drove off to a small restaurant with no name written not even on the menu, it had a beautiful garden view. Abuja hides so many gems like that. We sat down for an early dinner, the air thick with unspoken emotions.

It felt like a cloud of butterflies hovered above us. I couldn't explain it, but I was grateful for self-control and for a man with even greater self-control.

At that moment, there wasn't a single worry about the future. I loved how it felt, and I didn't care about tomorrow. Here and now was all that mattered.

"I love you, Saleem," I blurted, unable to hold it in.

He leaned close, as though to kiss me, but stopped. "I love you a lot more than you think" he continued "It just feels different. Wherever you've tied my heart, please keep the lid tight on that bottle," he teased.

I laughed, and his joke lightened the air, shifting the tension into something gentler, calmer.

We were literally the last people to leave the restaurant. We had ordered so much food and were unable to finish it, even though everything was delicious, so we packed everything to go. When we got to my place, we sat in the parking lot and talked some more.

I didn't realize Zainab had bombarded my phone and Saleem's with messages. When I opened my phone, I burst out laughing and quickly called her back.

"I don't blame you and Saleem! I planned the surprise and you people tossed me aside, like I didn't make this happen!" she exclaimed.

Saleem spoke up, "I thought I messaged you."

"I knew it! You are still with Hallittah. Is it not too late, you humans! By the way, Hallittah, has Saleem told you I am coming back to Nigeria next week? I doubt he did. Anyway, I am coming back to help ruin your moments since you both have side-lined me!"

I kept laughing and saying sorry to Zainab until she ended the call.

It was time to head inside. Saleem got out, carried the paper bags with our packed food, and walked me to my door. He gave them to me and whispered, "Good night. You are permitted to dream about me."

"It is not goodnight yet," I responded. "Let me know when you are home."

I showered and went to bed, ready to call Saleem to ask if he got home. I took a long bath, hoping he would have called, but he didn't. When I called, his line was busy. I waited until much later, and he called back.

"Hajiya just called me," he said.

For some reason, I wondered why Zainab and Saleem called their mum "Hajiya," but I guessed it was a name that stuck. I've seen Zainab also call her "Mama" but refer to her as Hajiya more often.

"When I came into town today, I called Ahmed to bring the car to me. He picked me up at the airport, I dropped him off close to the house and drove to see you. Hajiya saw him leaving the house. She found out I was back but was wondering why I didn't come home to greet them. So I just told her that I had so many things to handle, and I would see her in the morning. She didn't sound convinced," he laughed. "I will make it up to her."

"You should have at least gone inside the house to say hi to her before coming out," I said.

"She would have taken my time. I couldn't wait to see you. I had a great time tonight."

"I did too,". "I just showered and I would like to go through some paperwork and go to bed."

"I need to sleep as well," he responded. "I didn't sleep well yesterday, nor on my flight. I'm so surprised I am still vibrant."

"That is because you were high on vitamin Hallittah," I said.

He burst out laughing. "You are right, but I will shower soon and sleep now. I will see you tomorrow."

"Goodnight, Saleem."

"Night, Hallittah."

I woke up energetic the next morning. The boost I needed for life was back; everything felt like bliss. There was a troubling thought in my mind that I refused to give a voice. I was going to enjoy Saleem's company to the fullest, nothing mattered now.

My mum called me, bringing back a conversation I had ended some months back when Jason and I were still dating. I have always kept my conversations with her short to avoid her bringing it up again, but I knew this time I couldn't escape.

My dad and my mum had always supported my dreams and allowed me to choose a career of my choice and chase it to the fullest. Despite studying law, I chose to delve into business because I enjoyed the processes of helping businesses thrive as a developer. Despite this freedom, there were still issues surrounding my independence. Culturally, a woman should not leave her father's house until she is married, but it was different for me. I wanted what I wanted and always had my way, but I still had to answer to my mum, who kept bringing up conversations about marriage and the need for it. This call was exactly what I thought it would be.

"Hello Naima, hope you are fine. Your brother told me you moved to a new house. How is it going? Hope it is a safe place?" She didn't let me answer. "I was hoping you would be thinking of settling down instead of switching houses. What was wrong with that house that you left? It was very fine. When will you come home to visit?"

"Hopefully soon. I am trying to round up a project; when I am done, I will come home," I replied.

"Toh (ok), just make sure you are safe. Always come back to your apartment early to avoid staying out late. You are in my prayers may God keep you safe. I am heading to church soon."

"Thank you, Mum."

I ended the call. I was contemplating calling Saleem and wondering if he would be awake by this time in the morning. Then his call came in.

I answered. "I was just about to call you, wondering if you would be awake."

"I am awake," he responded. "Your line was busy. Who is the person who beat me to calling you this morning?" he asked. "Do I have competition?"

"That was my mum," I said.

"Oh, how is she?"

"She is fine."

"That's great. What are you up to next?" he asked.

"Just some paperwork, prepping for the next restaurant set up, I was hoping to leave for Lagos in a few weeks, after launching the Abuja restaurant."

"Alright, I will allow you do that. I will call you later; I need to go see Hajiya and Baba." (Baba is Ahmed's dad).

CHAPTER **7**

ocial media was becoming very prominent in the world and Nigeria, was not left behind. Part of my work is to also use it to influence the success of the restaurant. It was going to be the first to serve Korean-style dishes, and from the menu tasting we did at one of our meetings, some meals were spicy it would appeal to the Nigerian customers. But sustainability was key, and I also had to draft job descriptions for all the workers and the code of conduct. The setup was almost done. Even though this was the first restaurant gig I was handling, I was doing a pretty good job. In my previous consultancy jobs, I am used to a lot of paperwork, meetings, and back-to-back consultations. This was pretty easy, and I wanted to give it my best, since it was paying a nice return.

I loved the independence that comes with being a freelancer. I get to have enough time for myself and I pace myself. I make enough money to cater for myself, as I have been highly recommended. After meeting with Temi while I was in the United States, she said she was going to connect me with gigs in Nigeria and some multinational companies needing guidance into the Nigerian market. She was already doing that, so it meant more work and more pay for me.

There were times I considered job opportunities to grow in a company and climb the career ladder, but I always ended up turning down offers, most of which came from referrals. The pressure of an office setting didn't appeal to me much, but sometimes I craved the security it brings from the monthly salary and the bonuses.

I replied to emails, printed more paperwork, entertained some calls, and I was done for the day. By the time I was done, it was past 2 pm. I took a nap and woke up past 3:47 pm. I checked my phone and there was no message from Saleem, so I called Chiamaka.

"How is the Lagos traffic?" I asked as soon as she picked up.

"I can't relate; I live in VI. My place of work is 5 minutes away," she said.

I teased, "Big girl things."

"Yes oh! That is why parents ought to know sending your child to an expensive school is not a scam, the differences is always clear " she said.

The company provided Chiamaka with accommodation as part of her incentive. Chiamaka studied at Hult Business School for her MBA after her undergraduate degree in

Business from Oxford. When she came back, she was highly packed and ready for the Nigerian market. While others were leaving Nigeria to travel abroad to work, she always pointed out that it was better to work in Nigeria and get paid the same as any executive outside Nigeria, and I couldn't agree less.

"You should come visit soon," she said.

"I am definitely coming. Where do you think I will crash when I come to Lagos, if not your place?"

"You will love it. I am having a blast, even though the workload is kicking me in the butt now, but I hope it eases with time. You know how these things go."

"Yeah, you got this," I replied.

"How is your project coming along?" she asked.

"Great, we have made huge progress. We would be launching in a week if all goes well."

I was scrolling on my laptop when I received an email from Temi. She was asking if I could take on another project, and it made me happy that I had offers coming in. I got another job contract from her; I was going to look at it to see the timeline and expectations, if it was something I could take.

"Hello, are you there?" Chiamaka asked.

"Yes, oh, sorry. I got distracted by an email from Temi."

"I guess more work, right?

"Yes ooo"

"How is Saleem?" she asked. "You sound so happy, I know something great must have happened," she teased.

"I can't even hide my emotions from you, even when you are miles away," I said.

She laughed.

"He is back" I answered.

"Hmmm, take care of your heart, my love." she added, I know what she meant and I won't talk about it., "Anyway, bring all the gist from Abuja to Lagos with you when you are coming, I have ears for all the tea. I got so much work to focus on, talk to you later."

"Later"," I responded.

"Later" for us meant weeks to come, because we understood just how busy our work was. We spoke when we could and when a gossip deserved an SOS.

I decided to call Saleem as I hadn't heard from him.

"Hey, Hallittah."

"Hiya. You done with work?" he asked.

"Yeah, I didn't want to call you; I wouldn't want to interfere with your work."

"Oh, I'm done. It took a while, but I have wrapped up for the day."

"How is Hajiya and Baba?"

"They are well. I stayed longer when I visited to atone for not coming yesterday," he said in a sarcastic tone. "I got home a while back and did some work. I was going to call you much later. By the way, I have been writing when I was away, I bought two journals for you, at a street market it has an antic look for some reason; I believed you will like it; I knew I would see you again to give you."

"What have you been writing?"

"Rumi-inspired poetry," he replied.

"Can I read it?"

"Hmmmmm..."

"Come on," I pleaded.

"Sure, but you must promise not to laugh."

"I promised to laugh, if necessary," I replied.

"Then I don't think we have a deal."

"Ok, ok, fine. I would try not to laugh. Can I see it?"

"Sure, I will definitely bring it along. Can I call you back? Hajiya is calling." He excused himself and put me on hold to answer Hajiya's call.

Within a minute he was done. "Hajiya wants me to come again. I know it is nothing serious, but I better go. Once I am done, I will pass by yours before going home."

"Alright, later then."

I went to my kitchen to cook my hair concoction to keep myself busy: hibiscus, rosemary, neem, and fenugreek boiling on low heat. I would then simmer it and add honey as the last ingredient. I would use it to spray my hair and leave it in for some hours.

My phone buzzed. Saleem messaged that he might not be able to make it that evening to see me; his father needed him.

*Hope all is well?* I texted back.

*"It is fine, just paperwork and family stuff."*

*"Alright then. Let me get back to making my concoctions,"* I replied.

*"Keep some for me,"* he remarked slyly.

The following day, Saleem came in the evening, and we took a walk around the estate block.

"You seem to do well with setting up people's businesses. Have you ever thought of starting your own?" he asked.

"Yes," "but I never gave it much thought. Maybe a cafe but also a wellness centre where people can come, drink herbal teas, relax, get massages, sit in the garden and work.

It will be a quiet place, with soft piano playing, the same way it feels when you walk into a spa with Enya singing softly in the background. It will be a place where, if you're having a bad day, you could come and find a reason to feel better. You could sit alone, meditate, sit on the floor, or spend time in the garden. It will have a no-noise policy."

"Wow. And you should name it 'Hallittah'," he said.

"Hmm, never thought of it."

"You see why you need me in your life," he said "by the way Zainab is coming back in two days" I screamed in excitement.

I missed her so much. It's funny how you can meet someone only briefly and feel instantly attached. She carries this contagious energy sassy, outspoken, totally magnetic.

I've missed our gossip sessions. She always says I vibrate on the same frequency. With Chiamaka away in Lagos, Zainab's return couldn't be better timed.

"You don't have to say it," he gave me a playful shove. "You're excited she's coming back, aren't you?"

"Absolutely"

He laughed.

Whenever I take a walk alone, I get tired and never reach the estate gate, but I walked all the way with Saleem, and I didn't feel a thing. When we got back to my apartment, Hajiya called again and I had to say goodbye to him.

Since Zainab requested that Saleem and I pick her up at the airport, I thought of picking some flowers for her and our favourite pancakes. I wanted to see her reaction.

# CHAPTER 8

We got to the airport right on time, and in about 20 minutes she was walking out while two airport staff members helped with her cart, which was filled with her luggage . She ran and leapt into my arms; I clutched the flowers, fighting for balance as Saleem watched.

"If someone sees you both, they will think you're two long-lost twins who haven't seen each other in years," he said.

"I miss you too," she said, pinching Saleem on the stomach as he flinched in pain.

"You are back and you are already torturing me," he groaned.

She looked back at me. "Flowers, really Naima? I am just gonna act like it means the world to me," she said. She collected them and smiled. "Thanks for the colourful bushes."

We all cracked up laughing out loud.

"You have lived in America and still have not softened a bit. Why so much luggage? Are you packing your complete life from America?" Saleem asked.

She smiled and turned to me. "I've got gist for you, and I will need you to listen. Please, can you spend the night today in my house? I really need you." She turned to Saleem. "Stay away, by the way. I just need her for some weeks."

I laughed, sighing. "The pancake platters are in the car."

She giggled. "I knew it was a joke bringing some damn bushes, which I obviously love so much, by the way, but this is the real deal!" she said smiling mischievously, shoving some pancakes and strawberries in her mouth.

We had to stuff two extra luggage in the back seat. Saleem paid the two men that brought the cart out, and from the way they kept bowing and thanking him, it needed no telling that he gave them a lot of money.

As we pulled up their house, Hajiya came out smiling. Zainab jumped out and hugged her, Hajiya's face lit up with joy at the sight of her daughter. Soon, nearly every cousin streamed out some helping with Zanab's luggage, others simply calling out welcomes. Hajiya turned to me as I greeted her.

"Kin je ki kawo kawar ki ne?" (You went to welcome your friend?). her tone made It sound like a question, but I knew

Hajiya already knew I had gone with Saleem to pick Zainab up.

"Ee," (yes)I said.

Alhaji, Zainab's dad, had traveled outside of Nigeria, which meant fewer people for us to go greet. we rushed into Zainab's room for the gist she couldn't wait to divulge. Crashing on the bed, she hit me with the news, "I am getting married."

I squealed in excitement, but Zainab didn't seem too excited.

"What is wrong?" I asked.

She sighed. "Nothing bad, just scared. He is just like me, which is excellent because we are a rare breed on earth, but it scares me that we might not be able to complete each other in other ways."

"I think I understand what you mean, but can you dumb it down for me, madam Dr. Professor?" I teased her.

She let out a wide grin. "I love that title, by the way. I worked hard for it."

A knock on the door was followed by coolers and trays of food and drinks coming in. Hajiya had prepared almost every meal for Zainab. Zainab texted Saleem to come to her room. We opened the four coolers with smaller cookware with different delicacies. Saleem walked in.

"Not fair. I didn't get all this when I came back," he said.

Zainab stuck her tongue out at him.

"Anyway, Hajiya knows you have a tummy of a T-rex, the foodie of this house." He said

"Whatever," Zainab shrugged.

I chose tuwon shinkafa and miyan kuka, one of my favourite Northern meals. The miyan kuka is baobab leaf soup with tuwo, a rice meal that is cooked and turned into a dough-like consistency to be eaten with the soup.

Dinatu, the first-born child walked in. She was also married to a wealthy businessman and politician from Kano.

"Where is our Amarya?" she asked, referring to Zainab as the bride.

It turned out the news about Zainab accepting to marry Najeeb had already spread like wildfire. No wonder Hajiya had been so happy. Because no matter how we claim to be young women who have choices in modern-day Nigeria when it comes to marriage, it is every Northern woman's pride that her daughter gets married as early as 25. Now that Zainab is clocking 30, it felt like a miracle and prayer answered.

The room became lively with lots of chatter as we devoured every meal, while some of Dinatu's kids joined, hopping on Zainab with joy. It felt as though I was part of a big family myself; they had so much love amongst themselves.

I didn't realise Saleem was staring at me until Zainab cleared her throat. That's when I realised, and they all started laughing.

"Saleem, oh, make your move before a brother takes Hallittah away," Dinatu said carrying the last cooler of fried chicken out while her kids followed behind. I pretended like I didn't hear her say that.

Saleem got up and left with a plate filled with food, I turned to Zainab, she continued.

"Finally, everyone is gone. What I am trying to say is, marriage scares me a bit. What if he ends up wanting something softer than me?"

"Elaborate," I beckoned.

"Hallittah, you know what I meant. I know I am feminine, but not soft enough."

"Do you want to get married?" I asked.

She said, "Yes. He is handsome," she smiled. "Then Talk to him and find out more about what he is like."

"I think I know everything about him; we talk and video call a lot. It's just that... I feel he might want more."

"Well, you should stop assuming for him, except if he shows you otherwise. But I know what you mean. His exposure and his expectations, right?"

"Yes" she said

"He's seen you and talked to you, clearly, he likes what he's seen. I don't think you should worry. Not every woman is the same, you're beautiful besides" "worry about something else"

"How about we go to Amarya Veils and get all the Northern Women's secrets you know the spicy married-people knowledge. For the other room" I suggested.

She hugged me tight. "You see why I need you in my life? I never thought of that." Amarya veils teaches young women on how to handle intimacy and how to prepare for marriage.

"look, I know you have your rough edges, everyone does, but you are a smart beautiful, and logical woman. You'll have a good married life. I haven't met Najeeb, but I trust you are a good judge of character.

"Thank you, Hallittah. You are the sister I need at this crucial moment." She paused." Anyway, enough of this cheesiness. Let us draw an itinerary. And by the way, Najeeb is coming next week. I want to look beautiful to meet him. I am giving you the assignment to turn me into your beauty lab rat "

"Yes madam" I answered.

I was focused on rounding up the restaurant setup so I could spend more time with Zainab. The attention the restaurant is getting feels exciting. The first Korean restaurant in Abuja,

Nigeria, would be a success thanks to me. Once I am done with this stage, I have to create a blueprint that the restaurant will follow to keep the standards and not lose our customers.

In the morning, I woke up and rounded up some phone calls. Zainab was going to pick me up at the restaurant so we could go out for a girls' day out. I knew the next days would mean spending less time with Saleem, but I also knew he wouldn't be out of sight. I got to the restaurant and did my last check-up. Zainab's car drove in, and a smile lifted my face when I saw through the door that Saleem was the one driving.

Zainab walked in.

"Are you smiling for me or for Saleem?" she asked.

"For you, of course,"

"Liar," she said, pushing me slightly as I stood by the door, waiting for Saleem to come in.

"Hey beautiful."

"Hey," I smiled.

"You came."

He came close to my ear and whispered. "That's the only way I can get to see you now that Zainab is back."

Zainab shouted from the rear end, "I heard that!"

I took them around to see the progress we've made. "We're ready for the opening," I said.

"You did great Hallittah" Saleem said

"Halittah, I'm going to tell Hajiya that I'm going to Dinatu's house, but I'll come to yours instead. I'll tell Dinatu to cover up for me, so you can fix my life just like you did with this restaurant." I laughed

Most northern parents would not allow their young girls to leave home and stay on their own. But it's a decision I made for my self. I wanted to live my life how I deemed fit. I didn't want to get married without getting to achieve allot for myself. Besides, my parents don't even live in the same town as me, and I always craved independence. I want to work, earn and live. So, I understood why Hajiya might not accept Zainab staying at mine for days. So she lied.

She continued, "I cannot stay in that house. I barely get time to breathe."

"Of course, you know I want you around. Besides, there's so much that we need to do". "Najeeb is coming back this weekend," she smiled. "I miss him."

We left the restaurant and went straight to Sarauniya Kitchen, a restaurant that serves northern delicacies. The restaurant had an option of a seating area where we sat and eat on mats provided. Seating on mats is a Northern

Nigerian culture. Which is why Mats and Carpets are so common in most homes, just to seat and fold our legs.

All I wanted to eat was *miyan kuka* and *tuwon shinkafa* my absolute favorite. I could eat it every meal. I love Sarauniya Kitchen because she makes hers with chicken, and cow fat, that alone makes the food intoxicating. Soon our food was served, Saleem got the same food, while Zainab went for *miyan taushe* and *tuwon shinkafa. (Spinach soup and rice dough)*

We spent the evening bantering. This little union and friendship are healing my soul in ways I can't explain. I was lost in thought and didn't know Zainab and Saleem were staring at me. When I came back from the land of my lost thoughts, they both started laughing.

"Where did your mind travel to?"

"I smiled trying to fight the tears?"

"I just love you guys. I love this cycle."

"Awww," Zainab scurried over to hug me, staining my dress with her hand that had soup. I looked and saw she had a little tear in her eyes as well. Saleem just stared at us.

"Have you guys finished smearing yourselves with soup?" he asked, we shared a laugh.

# CHAPTER 9

After we were done eating, Zainab excused herself, leaving me and Saleem. He passed me a bottle of water.

"You didn't drink water since you started eating. Drink some."

It's the way he pays so much attention to me that makes me feel he might just be my soulmate.

Zainab came back.

"Let's go pack up from my house. I spoke to Dinatu, and I'll go tell Hajiya so I can spend the night at yours."

"Yay, girls' night! Girls' night!" I sang.

"Unfortunately, somebody is not invited," Zainab teased Saleem, who ignored us and went to pay the bills.

"If you guys keep dancing, I'll drive off and leave you here. Or better still, I'll tell Hajiya not to let you go."

"Hater!" Zainab responded.

The drive home was filled with Saleem and Zainab exchanging banter. I've always loved their sibling relationship; no one needs to tell you they are favorites to each other. We got to Zainab's home and greeted Hajiya.

"Dinatu said you're going to her house. Take some *kunun aya* (tiger nut milk) from the fridge to my grandkids," Hajiya said. "Saleem, carry some for yourself and hallittah as well." I thanked her.

It's more than obvious that Saleem is into me, the way Hajiya makes certain remarks and suggestions, it's clear she's in support of my relationship with him.

We drove to Dinatu's house and dropped the *kunun aya* that Hajiya sent to her grandkids, and we went straight to my house. Saleem didn't stay for long; he excused himself to go catch up on some work at home.

We spent the evening making different hair and body concoctions that are skin-friendly, honey scrubs with coffee and sugar, honey and black soap hair wash with blended rosemary. We took turns bathing hot showers that covered my bathroom with so much steam, enough to make a cloud. By the time we were done, we were so worked up I suggested applying pure cow fat oil on our skin and hair as it relaxes the body. We wore our robes and called Chiamaka.

Zainab had met Chiamaka a couple of times in the past. She picked up the call we switched to video a call.

Our smiling faces appeared on the screen.

"I'm jealous! You guys are shining like you bathed in baby oil.

"Cow oil," Zainab said.

"I'm jealous. As you can see, I haven't even removed the blouse I wore to work, and you guys are already chilling. I miss doing this."

"You should take a weekend off and let's chill," I suggested.

"It's not that easy, especially now that I'm trying to impress my boss at my place of work. Maybe much later, but now it's a little difficult to take a break."

"Sorry, ko," Zainab said, trying to pacify Chiamaka.

"Ladies, I have to leave you guys. I need to shower and sleep."

"Take it easy, ko," I added.

We ended the call and fell asleep. There's something cow oil and shea butter does to they body it gives deep instant relief, if massaged into the skin. I have always suggested for skin care and for body massage to get a good night rest, to get the complete benefit of having a nice hot bath and massage pure, unadulterated shea butter or cow oil on your skin. It seeps deep into the skin and eases tension.

Zainab woke up at dawn to pray and went back to bed. But I slept through until 9 a.m. we woke up very well-rested and hungry. We washed our faces, brushed, I whipped some pap while Zainab cut some yam, I fried it and we had it for breakfast.

I finally checked my phone, and as expected, a good morning text from Saleem since 7 a.m. was waiting. Smiling at my phone, Zainab stared at me with a smug on her face. "I don't want to even ask I know Saleem sent you a message."

I was replying to his text when Zainab's phone started ringing. She rushed and squealed with excitement.

"It's Najeeb!"

"Hmmm, imagine who is judging me, see how jumpy you are"

She picked the phone and went to the window. I watched as she tossed and turned on the phone, curling her toes. I knew my friend was in love. And as much as she acts all tough, deep down, I know she's a softy.

She ended the call while I stared at her, smiling.

"Don't judge me. I don't judge you and Saleem."

"You know that's a lie," I laughed.

"Whatever," she responded. "Guess what? Najeeb is in town, and he wants to have dinner with me, and you are coming!

He said I should bring you." She started dancing and screaming. Then she stopped. "Why am I acting this way?"

"Because you are in love."

"He said he wanted to surprise me but couldn't pull it off, so he couldn't help but tell me. He came into town this morning."

"What should I wear now?"

"You have so much to wear."

"But I don't think I have anything exquisite."

"You know that's a lie," I said.

We went through her box and decided on a black abaya dress with nice black beaded embroideries and stones.

I texted Saleem to come pick us up, and by the time he arrived, we were not ready we had spent so much time talking about men that we didn't know it was past 4:00p.m., and the dinner date was at 5:00p.m. when I opened the door for him to come in. He was holding some books.

"I got you more books," he said. I smiled, looking through them, Saleem has given me so many gifts that it feels as though I haven't matched one percent of it. I just have to think of something thoughtful to give him soon.

Zainab was done getting ready. I could smell my humra from her body as she stepped out. She texted Najeeb to tell him we were on our way, as he was already at the restaurant waiting for us.

It is rumoured that the Mai Rigas owned the fine dining restaurant we were going to and the five-star hotel beside it. We got in, and a smiling Najeeb was waiting for us. He held Zainab's hands and drew her to a seat.

"You must be Hallittah," he said, smiling, while keeping his eyes fixed on Zainab.

Saleem insisted on not following us inside. He told me he knew Najeeb since secondary school and he was his senior. And from the way he spoke of him, he had nothing negative to say.

Saleem drove off after dropping us. After a while, I wished I didn't come, not because Najeeb wasn't friendly, but because I felt I should give Zainab some space to catch up. I texted Saleem, who replied almost immediately:

*"I'm not far off; I can come pick you so we could hang around the mall until she's done."*

I agreed and excused myself, telling them I needed to attend to something. They couldn't persuade me to stay, so I left. Saleem picked me up, and we went to the mall.

I entered Azurfa, a jewellery store, and picked a silver ring for Saleem. Most northern men married or unmarried wear rings like a fashion statement. Saleem had one, which he wears once in a while. I got him a ring with a blue sapphire stone. I tried it on his finger, and when he realized I was getting him something, he insisted on paying for it. I refused, saying it was a gift. So, he got a silver necklace that had a blue sapphire stone on it for me.

We both paid for what we got and exchanged them. "You bought me a ring, do you want to ask me to marry you" I laughed "You know I won't say no right?"

We sat at the bookstore which also serves as a café on the basement floor of the mall.

"Zainab's in-laws visited yesterday," he said. "Her father-in-law came to see Baba in the house. Though the Mai Rigas and Saleem's family are not strangers to each other, the marriage between Zainab and Najeeb is going to make the families super close. She's going to get married soon, from the look of things. I'm very happy for her. Najeeb is responsible, I've never heard any scandal about him, and I believe he'll make a great partner for her."

He spoke with so much sincerity and hope for Zainab that I felt a wave of sadness on my face. The voice I had silenced came whispering again and this time, it was loud: *What will become of me and Saleem?*

We love each other, but that might not help in deciding what our future will be. He noticed my expression and changed the topic. Even though I smiled, deep down the war within had started. I had given that thought in my head a voice.

Zainab called to say that Najeeb was dropping her at mine, so we headed out. We got to my house and sat in the car in silence. Saleem drew back my chair to fall back, and he did the same. We lay there. Soon Zainab pulled up, holding so many gifts. Najeeb got down and exchanged greetings with Saleem.

"We brought you food since you refused to eat with us," Zainab said. "And Najeeb also bought some gifts for you."

I thanked him. I helped Zainab hold some items, we said goodnight to both Saleem and Najeeb and walked into the house, eager to hear how the evening went.

"Guess what! The Mai Rigas visited my family yesterday," Zainab said. "Najeeb asked if I don't mind them coming to start the introduction phase of our marriage."

"What did you say?"

"Of course, I said yes."

I opened the food they brought for me and began eating at the kitchen counter while Zainab opened her gifts excitedly.

She later sat beside me.

"You know Najeeb's dad married four wives. It's a big family. I'm just worried that it might be overwhelming."

"I told him, and he assured me it will be fine, as everyone minds their business. But he told me I should expect a lot of gossip and drama during the wedding, as celebrations in his family are a big deal. Najeeb's dad is also a Fulani man, and he married Najeeb's mother, who is Shuwa Arab. The Shuwa Arabs are a group of people with mixed Arab and indigenous African heritage. They have very distinctive physical features, a rich cultural history, and are native speakers of the Shuwa dialect of Arabic in Nigeria. I know for sure Najeeb's wedding would be a display of elegance and culture."

The day to finally open the restaurant came. So many reservations had been made, and I had to spend the whole day there. Zainab and Saleem were also around to support. I sat with them in a corner, watching the activities, taking notes, and occasionally visiting the kitchen to see how things were going.

I would go to Lagos next to ensure the launch of the restaurant there. Then, I could move on to other projects already waiting in line. From the look of things, with the projects lined up, I didn't need to be physically present just emails and phone calls, which used to be my normal routine. Even though the restaurant opening went well, I was eager to return to my regular work schedule.

Zainab's introduction day finally came. There wasn't much to do since the family handled everything. Even her dress was chosen by Hajiya. Zainab didn't care much about what to wear or how she looked. Hajiya has great taste, and we all knew she'd make Zainab look stunning. When she dressed up, the clothing and light makeup didn't disappoint, she looked stunning. Hajiya really knows what looks best on Zainab.

Najeeb, his father, and some of his relatives were seated in Baba's living room. Zainab was brought in by her mother. Her father asked,

"Are you aware of what is happening?"

"Yes," she replied softly, her head bowed.

"Did you tell these people to come and ask for your hand in marriage?"

"Yes."

"Is this what you want?"

"Yes."

"Mashallah," Baba said. "You can go."

Hajiya led her back into her room. Inside, her cousins and Dinatu were making joyful wedding sounds. I knew Zainab preferred quietness, but she endured the chatter of the happy aunties and cousins who wouldn't stop talking. Soon, the introduction was done.

Later, Najeeb texted her: *"You look beautiful today, just as always."*

She showed me the message, smiling shyly. He added that he would come to the house in the evening to see her. Now that it was official, Najeeb could visit her. Zainab told Hajiya about his visit, and when he came later that evening, he brought so many gifts in paper bags and nylon packs. I collected them and took them to her room while she sat outside with him.

When she came in, she sighed and said, "This feels unreal. I'm getting married."

"It will be perfect," I replied. "You'll make a beautiful wife."

Two weeks later, Najeeb's family brought her *sadaki* (dowry), so many boxes filled with clothes, wrappers, shoes, a makeup box, and even boxes of delicate underwear. Everything came in seven SUVs. I was expecting something grand, but this was beyond anything I had ever seen, it felt like the Mai Riga's were opening a market in Zainab's house. Her family gathered to collect the items.

Everything was packed into Hajiya's living room. Hajiya handled the purchase of all the custom-made outfits for the wedding. Zainab didn't have many friends, so I and her cousins made up her bridal train. The designer came to the house to take our measurements.

I spent most of the days with Zainab easing her tension, helping with preparations, and sometimes to escape to my house when the noise became too much.

When it was time for the *walima* (a prayer and send forth gathering for the bride), a female Islamic teacher, came to preach to Zainab about life in marriage. She spoke about love, patience, and intimacy, cracking jokes that had everyone laughing. By the end, there were tears, insights and lessons learned.

Then came the wedding ceremony, the dinner, and my favorite of all, the *kawyawa* party, where everyone dressed like villagers. It was so much fun! It reminded me of the first event I attended during Zainab's brother's wedding, when we first became friends. The outfits, the music, and the energy were all breathtaking. The *Mai Rigas* brought their A-game, and many prominent Nigerians attended.

On the last day, we took Zainab to her matrimonial home. She was covered in a light veil, and when she left home, she cried. Even though she wasn't moving far, it was an emotional moment. Baba kissed her forehead and prayed for her, with tears in his eyes. Hajiya was overwhelmed too.

# CHAPTER 10

Dinatu, Zainab, and I rode together while Saleem drove. Other family members followed in the convoy. It was late in the evening. I held Zainab's hands tightly as they were trembling. I knew she was anxious.

When we got to Najeeb's house, it was obvious it had just been built, a gift from his father to him and Zainab. We took her inside and sat her on the bed. She held my hands and didn't want to let go. We both cried like we wouldn't see each other again.

"Thank you," she whispered, tears in her eyes.

Then Najeeb came in and whispered something to her that made her chuckle. That small laugh gave me peace I knew she had married right. I left the room and found Saleem waiting in the car, emotions written all over his face. Everyone loved Zainab.

After Dinatu left, Saleem drove me home. I told him to come in, and he did. We sat on the kitchen counter in silence for a while.

"You know we can't keep avoiding the obvious, right?" I said, looking straight into his eyes. Normally, I couldn't hold his gaze for long, but this time I wanted him to see that I meant every word.

"I never knew what broken heart syndrome was Saleem, not until I found out, with me as the lab rat in the experiment. If I'm cautious now about love, about men, about the future, it's because I've learned what to avoid. I love you. But our tomorrow looks like chaos."

Saleem picked up one of the books he had gotten me a translation of Rumi by Rafic Abdullah and began to read:

"I have a thirsty fish in me
that can never find enough
of what it's thirsty for.
Show me the way to the ocean!
Break these half-measures,
these small containers.
All this fantasy and grief.
Let my house be drowned in the wave
that rose last night in the courtyards
hidden in the center of my chest.
Abdullah is the lamp,
I am the crazed, weeping heart."

"The poem speaks of the uncontrollable nature of the heart shattered by love," he said.

I watched him and imagined us old and grey, sitting on a porch while he read to me, his Hausa accent soft beneath his English words. But I wouldn't let myself drift into fantasy. Not this time.

"You should have told your parents poetry was what you wanted to study, not computer science," I said.

He laughed, and the tension dissolved a little.

"Silly goose," he said. "They wouldn't disown me. Besides, the first Rumi book I ever read was from my father's library."

Saleem caressed my palms. Tears welled in my eyes.

"I see pain before it happens. I guard my heart before doom comes. Saleem, we're going to be a problem to each other in the future. We need to let go."

"I know your fears," he said. "I have them too. But because I'm a man, I feel I can protect you from the drama of the future. I can assure you peace, love and unwavering commitment, even when it hurts. Maybe I don't fully understand what you see, but I understand enough to know I don't want to lose you."

"Goodbye is going to hurt," I said softly.

He sighed. "Is this really a breakup? Can't we just find a way? You go to church; I go to the mosque. I promise not to cross paths with your faith or disturb your practice. I can make it work."

"Saleem," I said quietly, "marriage in this country isn't just about two people. It's about families. If we leave this country, maybe it would work. But if I told my mother with her fragile heart that I want to marry a Muslim... I could lose her. After losing my dad, she's become even more delicate. The church, the community they won't let her rest. And I want a love that's spiritually yoked where we can hold hands in the morning and pray together."

He nodded, pain clouding his face.

"I knew this day was coming," I said, "I just didn't want to believe it."

He held my hands tightly. "You're breaking my heart again. But I can't blame you."

"I have to go," he said, standing up. "Call me if you need me."

I followed him to the door.

"Please," I whispered, "make it easy for me."

He smiled faintly. "You should finish that book you started writing about us. I'll miss you. I'll try to give you space, but I won't stop loving you. That's something I can't undo."

He kissed my forehead and left.

I sat on the floor and wept.

I sat for a while by the doorposts; the feeling burned slowly, like a slow descent into hell. My chest thumped heavily. "It's time to leave Abuja," I told myself.

That night, I packed my things and texted Amaka, *I'm coming to Lagos. I'm about to book my flight.*

She responded with her address.

I booked a morning flight, but when morning came, I postponed it and rebooked for an evening one. Then I texted Saleem, *I'm going to Lagos for some time. I know I'm not supposed to message you, but I just felt I should let you know.*

He called as I pressed the sent button.

"Can I take you to the airport at least, since your flight is in the evening. Let me take you to lunch, spend the day with you, and I'll drop you off at the airport."

I agreed. Twenty minutes later, he was at my house. He helped me carry my luggage to his car, and we drove off to Moeshen Café. We sat outside. I remembered our iconic date here, the laughter, the way he looked at me.

We didn't talk about the breakup. Instead, Saleem cracked jokes, telling stories from his childhood, silly memories of Zainab, like when she poured a whole cup of Vaseline on herself and dusted it with baby powder.

I texted Zainab: *Emergency. I have to go to Lagos for work. I'll be back soon.* I called her, but she didn't pick up.

We spent hours at the café before heading to the airport. In the car, Saleem played a song, a country tune I hadn't heard before.

"Who's this?" I asked.

"Brad Paisley," he said. "The song's called *She's Everything.*"

"My dad loved gospel country music," I smiled. "It's been a while. Country songs remind me of home. The words always make sense."

I leaned back in my seat and listened to Brad Paisley's album as we drove. I was so carried away that I didn't notice when Saleem tapped me gently.

"I want to intentionally make you miss your flight," he said softly, "but I can't."

I jolted up, realizing it was almost time. I ran into the departure terminal D. I was the last passenger to check in. I made it just in time, fighting my tears as I found my seat.

This was my reality now; to love and to lose.

The one-hour flight to Lagos was quiet. I thought about my life, the relationships that never made it, the pieces of me left behind with every goodbye. Maybe I should take a break from dating though I never believed in it. But maybe this time, it's what I need.

I thought about my future how it always included falling in love, having kids, and living in a homestead with a big garden. I used to imagine my little ones playing in the sand, laughter echoing through the air. A home with a wide kitchen where I'd cook, mix herbs, and make tea.

But now, I've added another dream: a large window overlooking the garden, a soft chair by its side, where I could write. I want to write books, romantic books for girls like me and men like Saleem. For people made for love.

To be honest, I don't know what to do with this soul of mine that beats to love someone. I wasn't made to be alone. I was made to pour into someone to love deeply and be vulnerable. I know good men exist, but I don't know if anyone can ever beat Saleem at this. He has set the bar high. I'm cooked.

When I got to Chiamaka's apartment, she'd already informed the security guard to let me in and left the key behind a flower vase. Zainab's call came in almost immediately.

"Hallittah, I've been sick," she said weakly. "My husband insists I rest. The wedding stress got to me. But I need to talk to you alone. Can you speak?"

"Yes, I'm alone," I replied.

"I'm anxious," she confessed. "Najeeb and I haven't consummated our marriage. He just holds me to sleep. I think my anxiety is making me sick. I overthink everything it gives me migraines."

I laughed lightly.

"Are you laughing at me?"

"No, dear. It just sounds funny because I understand."

She sighed. "All the lessons the women gave me before marriage didn't help. I was bathed in herbs, massaged with oils until my skin softened. They made me teas, drinks even smoked me with incense. They said it would prepare me, make me attractive to him. But now... I freeze when he gets close. I start trembling. I don't want him to get tired of me rejecting him. He's been so patient."

I could hear her crying.

"Stop crying," I said. "Where's Najeeb?"

"He stepped out."

"Good. Take a deep breath. Go shower. Use the lavender oil and shea butter I made for you."

"Okay, I'll find it."

I waited on the phone until she did.

"Now apply it your body, feet, ears. Wear your lingerie, your see-through nightwear. Breathe, Zee. Remember, Najeeb knows beneath that bold woman is a sweet, shy girl. He won't judge you. Just calm down. Make tea. When he returns, talk to him. Hold his hand. Bury your face in his lap if you have to. Just talk."

"Thank you, Hallittah," she said quietly. "I love you."

I settled into Chiamaka's apartment, fighting the urge to text Saleem to say I'd arrived safely. But that would mean holding on. I needed to let go for both of us.

Chiamaka came in an hour later with food. She hugged me tightly.

"I brought food," she smiled. "You'll love it."

We sat on the floor and devoured the meal.

Later, we talked about Lagos traffic, her work, and the restaurant opening. She avoided the topic of Saleem intentionally.

That night, I slept as soon as my head hit the pillow. My mind and body had been waiting to shut down.

The next morning, Chiamaka left early for work.

"won't you eat breakfast" I asked

"You know my job gives us breakfast and coffee," she teased.

"You proud goat," I laughed.

"Yes, oh!" she shouted as she left.

I smiled. She deserved all the good things coming her way.

I headed to the restaurant site. Everything was almost done only finishing touches left. Lagos, the city of lights and chaos, was ready for the new branch. I was relieved when the CEO suggested someone else handle Port Harcourt. That meant I could finally rest.

Chiamaka helped promote the opening, six of her colleagues made reservations for the opening night. The restaurant opening night finally came, everything buzzed with life. I monitored with my pen and paper like always, writing everything that would need to be revised.

One more guest arrived, it was a friend of Miles Chiamaka's colleague who just came into town, named Chisom.

He sat beside me. "You're the one running this place, right?"

"Not really," I smiled. "Just setting it up."

We got talking. He was warm, funny, easy. He told me he co-owned a fintech company and danced salsa and a part of an Afro-Latin dance community in Abuja. It felt as though he was divulging too much information about himself.

He reminded me of an old chapter of my life, with Jason, of dance classes I never went back to.

Chisom was nice. But I wasn't ready. I'm tired of giving pieces of myself away, I am not ready for anything, not even a friendship.

We exchanged numbers anyway.

That day when we got back to Chiamaka's apartment, I sat quietly in the living room while she showered and went to bed. I told her I needed to catch up on some work, but the truth was I just needed to sit alone with myself.

I cried.

I missed him.

I missed Saleem.

I wondered how he was coping, what he was doing, if he was okay. The ache in my chest grew unbearable, so I lay down on the couch and whispered a silent prayer:

*Dear God, help me ease this pain. Give me peace. Direct my path.*

My dad would often say that sometimes, we go through pain so we can draw closer to God. Maybe he was right. At that moment, I didn't know what else could soothe my heart except prayer. I must have drifted off while crying, because the next thing I heard were Chiamaka's footsteps coming from her room. I hadn't realized I'd fallen asleep.

I told myself I needed to visit my mum. I missed home. Ever since my dad died, home hadn't felt the same and I hadn't been fair to her. I'd drowned myself in work, or in my own thoughts, always preferring her to visit me instead. Still, I made sure she had everything she needed: her favorite teas and coffees, essentials stocked in storage, and a monthly allowance. She's still a civil servant, but I ensured she lacked nothing.

Apart from constantly reminding me about marriage, she's always been grateful for how I take care of her. She spends most of her time in church praying, helping the caretakers clean, or attending numerous women meetings in church. My mum is a true prayer warrior.

So my decision to stay away from Saleem was not just about me, it was about her too. I love my mum deeply. Losing my dad was hard enough; I couldn't bear to break her heart. It's been barely three years since he passed.

CHAPTER

I told Chiamaka I'd be returning to Abuja that week to prepare for my trip home to Gombe. I made breakfast that morning. Then Miles called, insisting he wanted to visit. We both knew his persistence had more to do with Chisom than with us, and Chiamaka wouldn't stop teasing. We told the guys to bring along some drinks and snacks.

When the bell rang and I opened the door, I was stunned by the amount of snacks and drinks they carried.

"Miles, you've never visited me before. What's going on?" Chiamaka asked from behind.

He laughed. "Ah, Chiamaka, you know I just care too much about you."

"Shift jor," she replied, laughing. "I know Chisom put you up to this."

Chisom and I set up the snack table while Chiamaka got some ice for the drinks. We played a card game where everyone had to answer questions or perform tasks. One of the cards said everyone should sing a country song.

Chisom sang *When I Get Where I'm Going* by Brad Paisley and Dolly Parton. His voice was soulful, the song, reminded me of the one Saleem played the day he dropped me off at the airport.

"You listen to Brad Paisley?" he asked.

I nodded. "Just recently. A friend introduced me."

I smiled remembering a beautiful memory. "My dad loved country music too. He always played cassettes on his old radio when I was little."

Miles then broke into another song with a funny lyric he sang, *Your New Boyfriend Is Ugly and I am glad that he is*, we all laughed. The night was light-hearted and warm.

Later, Chiamaka and Miles went out to buy suya, leaving me alone with Chisom. It felt like a setup, and Chiamaka's playful glance confirmed it. I nodded, letting her know I was fine with it. Before they left, I reminded them to get the suya meat with a little fat on it. Chiamaka already knew my rule.

"You're one interesting woman," Chisom teased. "Most women avoid fat, but you prefer it."

I laughed. "I love the taste of it. I eat healthy, so a little fat once in a while won't hurt."

"Interesting," he said, smiling.

"I'm heading back to Abuja Wednesday or Thursday," I told him. "I want to go and get ready to visit my mum in Gombe. It's been a while."

"Oh, nice. Hopefully I'll see you in Abuja then. Maybe I'll invite you to a dance class if you're up for it."

"Sure," I replied. "Let's see how it goes."

We talked about our families. He told me his mother was a retired professor of history from University of Nigeria, Nsukka, and his father a retired General. I could tell he adored his mother. For some reason, I let my guard down. Maybe because he liked Brad Paisley and Saleem did too.

"What do you do for fun?" he asked.

"I love making herbal concoctions for hair and body," I said. "I mix oils and create blends for health and wellness. My mum taught me some things, but my grandpa really sparked my curiosity. He once used python fat as a healing balm for my aunt, and it worked. When we were kids, he'd make this bitter herbal mixture called *madachi* whenever we had stomach aches it tastes awful, but it worked instantly."

"Interesting," Chisom said. "My dad has this recurring leg pain. Maybe you could make a balm for him. I'll pay."

"Sure," I smiled. "When I get back to Abuja, I'll make something for him."

When Chiamaka and Miles returned with the suya and bread, we all ate together and laughed late into the night. After they left, Chiamaka wouldn't stop teasing me about Chisom's interest, but I brushed her off.

I booked my flight for Wednesday, said my goodbyes, and flew back to Abuja. All I wanted was to see Saleem.

Zainab came over not long after I got back. She looked radiant, more relaxed and beautiful.

"Marriage life suites you" I teased, she smiled.

Najeeb had bought her a car and also got her a driver. She bought me some head scarf s and a dress.

"By the way," she said, "since you left, I've only seen Saleem once. He didn't look depressed, but he looked like someone drenched with ice water in winter. Something is wrong, but I won't pry.

Are you okay?"

"I'm fine," I answered softly. "I just want to prepare to go home to Gombe to see my mum. I'll spend this week shopping before I leave."

"How's married life?" I asked.

"Great," she said with a smile. "My in-laws are nosy, but Najeeb warned them not to visit without calling first. I'm sure they'll gossip about it, but I don't care. Funny thing is, he didn't even tell me, he just told them directly. They came over last week without notice, ate and chatted, and then he asked the driver to take them home. He told them next time to call before coming. I love that man."

She paused and looked at me. "As much as I love you and Saleem, I'd hate to see either of you hurt. If you're not meant to be, God will bring better partners for you both. You two have the biggest hearts I know."

After she left, I felt a nudge to start writing again. I went to the supermarket, bought new journals and books on creative writing, and continued reading some of the books Saleem had gifted me.

Later, Zainab messaged me:

*Saleem is doing okay. He sends his regards and gave me some books for you. I'll send the driver to drop them off.*

I went shopping and packed a box of clothes and provisions for my mum and cousins. I didn't forget to bring a box filled with chocolates and sweets. I always make sure my mum never runs out, because during Sallah celebrations, Christmas, and New Year's, kids from our area come to our house to greet her and receive treats. It's a tradition here: children go house to house, collecting cash gifts and edibles. And since my late father was known as *Mai Bishara* (the preacher) we always get more than our share of visitors.

I chartered a car from the park to take me from Abuja to Gombe.

Harmattan was already setting in across the northern part of Nigeria. This has always been my favourite time of the year. It was November, the ember months, a season that always came with a certain bliss. The weather was perfect: cold and windy in the mornings, slightly hot in the afternoons, and colder again by evening.

I remember as a child, we would start a fire early in the morning to keep warm. After sweeping the compound, we used the fallen leaves and dry branches to set up the fire. Almost every nook and cranny of the village had a fireplace when we visited our grandparents in Kaltungo. The older cousins told stories with songs around the flames.

There was this huge mountain whose view could be seen from my grandfather's compound. It stood in a faraway village, yet so tall that we could see its outline clearly. The mountain was shaped like a human face. My cousin once told me that, in the olden days, the mountain belonged to a huge snake that protected the community during wars.

The story went that the chief priest would hold a calf or sheep, while mothers and children followed behind. When they reached the mountain, the priest would push the calf inside. The snake would eat it and vacate the cave for the villagers to hide inside. Then the last person to enter the cave would bring another calf at the far end of the mountain for the snake to eat again. After that, the warriors would wear red ropes on their trousers to distinguish themselves from their enemies, they would go to war. The snake would join them, kill the enemies, and return to the mountain once victory was secured, by that the villagers inside the cave would go back to their home's. It was said that the village never lost a battle; the snake was the community's secret protector.

As we drove through Kaduna, Jos, and Bauchi, and finally entered Gombe State, I felt a wave of nostalgia wash over me. I hadn't told my mum I was coming that day, I only informed her that I would come soon. I wanted to surprise her. When I arrived home around 5 p.m., I found her sitting under the tree near the car park with her Bible in hand.

She sprang up as soon as she saw me. "You didn't tell me you were coming today!" she said, hugging me tightly.

"I wanted to surprise you," I laughed.

The truth is, if my mum knows I'm coming, she'll call a million times. Sometimes it gets overwhelming. She always wants to know where I am at any given time.

After we put my luggage's away, she quickly brought out her food flask so we could eat together tuwon *shinkafa* with *soboroto* soup. It had enough groundnut paste and spring onions, just the way I like it.

I brought her so many gifts and watched in excitement as she opened them one by one. The evening ended in tears when she brought up my late dad. It's a topic that will always make us emotional. My dad was our everything. Home was never the same after he died.

He was the kind of northern father who doted on his daughter. He sent me to the best schools and taught me to dream big. While other fathers saw marriage as the ultimate achievement for their daughters, mine believed a woman could be more than just a wife. He always told me to keep God constant in everything I do. That night, Mum and I drank tea in his honour.

Before we slept, she said softly, "I know I bug you about marriage, but I want you to marry right and marry well. It's better to marry late than wrong."

The next morning, I sat on the veranda with my journal and began to write. I poured my emotions onto paper, sometimes fighting back tears as memories flooded my heart. The weather was perfect dusty, calm, and cold.

After breakfast, I took a walk to visit our neighbours. In our community, every child belonged to everyone. I was that child loved and nurtured by many. My dad, being a preacher, was highly respected, and expectations for me as the first child were always high.

I stopped by the home of my childhood friend, Hadiza. We had an unbreakable bond growing up. The only thing that separated us was religion, I attended Sunday school, and she went to *Islamiyya* (Islamic school). We often slept in each other's homes.

But life took us apart when I left Gombe for university. She had an accident and died in her first year. Every time I visited her family, her mother cried. This time, when I arrived, she hugged me tightly and called to her husband, "Naima ta dawo!" (Naima is back!)

Her father, now older and walking with a cane, came out smiling. "We thought you wouldn't come back to this town," he said.

"I always wanted to," I replied. "Work just got overwhelming."

When I noticed his leg, I suggested they visit a private hospital in town and assured them not to worry about the bill. Mama Hadiza started crying. "I have always told people my daughter isn't dead," she said. "That God gave me another daughter."

She prayed for me with tears in her eyes: "May God bless you with a good husband, a compassionate man who will take care of you."

Before I left, she gave me a huge basket of soursop from her backyard. I arranged for a driver to take them to the hospital the next day and promised to check up on them frequently.

Being home began to heal me. On some evenings, I walked barefoot through our compound, plucking ripe oranges and mangoes as I went.

My neighbours brought food daily, and the house felt alive again. Slowly, I started to forget about Saleem. I poured myself into writing and revived my children's book club, something I used to do for the kids in the community.

Soon, about thirty-five children gathered every evening. We read *Queen Premier*, and storybooks. Their laughter filled the air making me feel a complete sense of fulfilment.

One evening, my phone rang it was Chisom. I saw his missed calls some days back. I had texted him earlier but never called back.

Before he said anything, I laughed, "I know, I owe you a call."

He chuckled. "You must have been busy in your hometown. Your friend Chiamaka told me you were there. I was hoping to see you in Abuja."

"I'm loving it here," I said. "My kids are coming soon for their lessons."

"Kids?" he asked, surprised. "You have children?"

I laughed. "Not biological kids, but some children in my community. I teach them how to read and write."

He exhaled. "Whew! You scared me for a second."

His humour was refreshing.

A few days later, he called again. "I was passing by the mall and saw some books your kids might like," he said. "Before you say no, I already bought them."

"Thank you. I'll send the driver's I use so you can send them through him."

When the books arrived, I was speechless there were so many. I called him immediately. "This is too much! The kids will love it."

"It's nothing," he said softly. "Call me later, I'm stepping into a meeting."

We began speaking more frequently. His kindness reminded me of Saleem except that Chisom was more vocal, while Saleem always carried a calm, quiet strength.

Before I knew it, December came. I had to return to Abuja. I said my goodbye to my mum and arranged for a Youth Corp member serving in my state to take over the book club, I will be paying her monthly. Home had truly rehabilitated me. For the first time since my father's death, it felt warm again.

When I arrived, I gave a cleaner access to my apartment through Zainab who made sure everything was spotless. I walked in, exhausted but thankful. Then my eyes fell on the books Saleem had bought for me, neatly stacked on the kitchen counter. A sharp pain cut through my heart.

I showered and tried to sleep but woke up around 3 a.m., restless. I began sorting through the local herbs and oils I brought from Gombe, the black soap, kernel oil, hibiscus, rosemary, and dried leaves for tea.

The next morning, I woke up to missed calls two from Zainab and one from Chisom. I called Zainab first; she was already on her way to see me. Chisom wanted to meet later that day, but I felt too tired. I didn't want to turn him down, yet I wasn't ready to share spaces that reminded me of Saleem.

Zainab arrived, eyes bright. "Guess what?"

"You're leaving Nigeria?" I teased.

"No, silly! I'm pregnant!" she shouted, grinning from ear to ear.

"Oh, my goodness!" I screamed, hugging her tightly. "I'm so happy for you." Tears filled my eyes.

"Najeeb didn't even want me coming here, but I had to tell you in person," she laughed.

"How's Saleem?" I asked quietly.

"He's okay, I guess. Hardly see him these days. I think he's traveling to the U.K. soon. You know what let's all meet up. I bet he'd love that."

She called him; he didn't pick up. But when she texted and told him I was with her he replied instantly: *'Okay, see you soon. What time?'*

I rolled my eyes, laughing. "You see? He replied faster because he heard you are coming."

Zainab frowned playfully. "He'll hear from me today."

I showered, tied my hair neatly, and wore my favourite abaya with the silver slippers Zainab got me from the U.S.

# CHAPTER 12

When we arrived at the café, Saleem was already there in a white kaftan. He smiled when he saw us.

Zainab scolded him playfully. "You don't pick my calls, but the moment you heard Hallittah was coming, you replied with lightning speed!"

He laughed and held her hands. "I'm sorry," he said sincerely.

We all laughed.

After a while, Najeeb called, and Zainab excused herself. Saleem looked at me quietly. "I missed you, Hallittah. It's been torture not being close to you. I think of you... of us all the time. I just didn't want to make it harder."

I smiled. "I understand. It's nice to hear you say it. I miss us too."

He cleared the bill, and Zainab suggested he drive me home. The ride was quiet, "This is awkward."

He smiled. "Very awkward. But I like it. I love your company."

He dropped me off, waved goodbye, and drove off. That simple meeting left me smiling all night. I didn't want anything to spoil that peace, so I called Chisom to cancel our meeting.

I had rescheduled my meeting with Chisom for the next day We met at a lounge close to my house.

"Finally," he said upon sighting me, smiling.

"It's nice to see you again," I replied.

"Hallittah, you are one special woman," he said warmly.

I smiled. "By the way," he continued, "I've been meaning to ask; Hallittah sounds very northern. What does it mean?"

"I think it means *creation*," I said, "but it's spelled a little differently from the original Hausa spelling, *Halittah*."

"Well, God sure does create," he said with a grin. "Do you only answer to Hallittah?"

"People from home call me Naima, it was a name given to me by my grandfather."

"I love Naima," he said softly. "I think I'll just keep calling you that."

I smiled.

"Thank you so much for the books," I said. "The kids loved them. You really put a smile on their faces. I'm grateful, we all are."

"Don't mention it," he replied. "It's nothing."

He leaned back. "Do you miss home?"

"Yes, actually, I do. This last visit was different. Unlike most visits, it was refuelling. It was something I needed to carry on with life. I'm glad I went."

"Well, I'm glad you had that time," he said. "I've never really taken a break, but one place I'd love to visit someday is Bali."

"Me too," I said, smiling. "I've heard it's beautiful I've seen pictures."

"If I ever take a break," he said, chuckling, "I'll go there for two weeks, switch off my phone, and just hope my company doesn't burn down by the time I'm back."

"I doubt it will," I said. "You seem like a man who's crossed his T's and dotted his I's. I bet it will survive your absence"

"Well, I'm glad you see me that way," he said, smiling. Then, after a pause, he added, "I don't mean to scare you or chase you away, but I really like you. Please pick my calls after now. I'm not rushing you or anything I just want you to get to know me, grade me, and accept me if I meet the cut off point."

I laughed. I knew he liked me, obviously, but I wasn't expecting it to come out of his mouth this quickly.

"I'm actually on a relationship detox," I said, "taking a break. I need more space for me and my thoughts."

"I understand," he said. "I promise not to bug you. But would you make room for a friend at least? I promise not to overstep my boundaries."

"I think we're already friends," I replied.

"Well, that's great to hear," he said with a grin. "Now that we're friends, can I invite you to a salsa class? You'll love it."

"Let's see how the week goes," I said.

"I'll call and pick you up when you are ready".

Honestly, I needed to go out more often, to ease up the gloom. Dating Chisom wasn't an option, but I didn't mind having a social life.

I decided to give a day out a chance, Chisom picked me up from home. The class wasn't bad at all. I learned how beautiful salsa is. The lead, often the man, guides the woman, known as the follow. I lost count of how many times I stepped on Chisom's feet, but he was patient and good at it. After a few dances, I loosened up, and he said I was a fast learner. We began speaking more frequently and grew a genuine friendship.

One evening, after work, we went for the dance socials where every dancer comes out to showcase their moves. I was seated watching, while Chisom got me a mocktail. My heart dropped when I heard, "Naima." The familiar voice needed no introduction it was Jason.

Chisom noticed the sudden change in my mood as I turned to face him.

"Hi, Jason," I said.

"Long time," he said, stepping closer as if to hug me. I extended my hand instead.

"This is the last place I'd think to see you," he said.

I smiled faintly. Chisom held my hand. "Meet Chisom," I said. Jason shook his hand.

"Well, it's nice seeing you again," Jason said before walking away.

I felt cold. Chisom asked if I wanted to leave, but I insisted on staying. After a while, I asked him to take me home.

On the way, I told him about Jason how I had forgiven, even forgotten, but the memories still hurt. Tears welled up in my eyes as I remembered the heartbreak, the trauma, the pain. Then I thought of Saleem how he had healed me with an affection I had never felt before. I couldn't help it. I fought so hard, but my emotions got the best of me, and I cried.

Chisom held my hand, wiping my tears. I was so vulnerable; I didn't realize how much I had been holding in. The breakup with Saleem was still hard.

He held my face in his hands and wiped my tears gently. I looked into his eyes and saw something genuine the warmth of true friendship.

"I don't think I'm your type of person," I said softly. "Sex isn't an option for me in relationships. I guard my body with utmost care. I've dated men who respected that, and I'm not about to change."

"Is that the only condition?" he asked.

"There are others," I said, "but this one is non-negotiable."

"I can do that," he said confidently.

"Are you sure?" I asked.

"That's not a problem. Trust me."

I smiled.

As I got out of the car, he asked, "So, can I call you *my Ima*?"

"What does that mean?" I asked, laughing.

"You know," he said, "I took 'Na' from your name and added 'my' so, *my Ima*. Can I?"

"Sure," I said.

"Yes!" he shouted with excitement.

I felt safe with Chisom, but I couldn't help comparing him to Saleem. I wished it was Saleem. I wished it was him I was with. Now, I had to go through the slow process of getting to know someone else again. Chisom gave me a sense of familiarity he was someone I could see a future with.

When he invited me to his church, on Sunday, I felt a deeper reason to trust him.

Our relationship was different from what I had with Saleem. I was now with Chisom, but whenever I wrote poetry, I still wrote about the feelings I felt when I was with Saleem.

I called Zainab so we could hang out, but she insisted we meet at her at home instead. When I arrived, she stared at me deeply.

"You look glowy, a lot better than when you came back from home," she said.

I smiled. "I met someone, his name is Chisom."

"Oh, wow. Now I want to hear all about it."

"He's nice and kind," I said, "but he's not like Saleem."

She looked at me knowingly. "I don't think you'll ever meet someone like Saleem. And the same goes for him he won't meet someone like you. No one can be you, Hallittah. You're made uniquely as you. So please, don't compare this experience with Saleem or anyone. Be with Chisom for who he is. You said he's a nice guy, give the nice guy a chance."

She smiled. "As much as I want you and Saleem for each other, I don't want either of you hurt. I don't want to choose sides."

"Enough about me," I said. "How are you feeling? Do you feel pregnant angry, sleepy, hungry, or tired?"

She laughed. "Najeeb is out of Nigeria. He didn't want to go, but I urged him to. It's a business trip. He'll be back next week. I don't want him staying home because of me."

"You married right, my dear," I said.

She smiled. "And you will marry right too."

I left Zainab's home happy with a stomach filled with cooked meals.

I made a healing balm for Chisom's father a mixture of castor oil, shea butter, castor oil, and neem oil. I told him that after a hot bath, his father should be massaged with the balm.

Chisom later called, saying his father slept through the night and felt less stiffness and pain. That feedback made my day. I always say that medicine and traditional remedies should go hand in hand, they should lean into each other.

That evening, Chisom came over. We sat on the carpet, drinking tea I had made with ginger, milk, and cardamom. He played a song on my MP3, *You're My Kind* by Seal. Then he nudged me to stand.

I got up reluctantly as he held my hands and pulled me close. We swayed gently to the song, my head resting on his shoulder. He moved slowly with me, the music wrapping around us. That little moment of intimacy changed a lot between us.

The song played on repeat. When the song ended, he said goodnight and left.

We spoke on the phone all through his drive home.

I want to move on. I know I could if only I could stop judging myself, stop telling myself that being with someone new means I'm cheating on Saleem. We're no longer together, yet the lingering feeling clings to me.

That afternoon, I decided to call Zainab, just to check on her, but she didn't pick up.

The year was fast coming to an end. I had made enough money from the deals I'd taken on, yet an emptiness swept over me from time to time, leaving me feeling like nothing I did was worth anything. It felt as though life was moving left, not forward.

I knew I had to find meaning again. Chiamaka would probably suggest therapy, but I wanted to do what my father always told me to do whenever life felt too heavy to carry, "*pray first, before anything else,*" he will say.

It had been a while since I went to church. I still said short prayers at home, but deep down, I knew that kind of devotion wasn't enough. I love God with all my heart. One of the reasons I couldn't be with Saleem was because of our different beliefs and I knew it might cause conflict eventually.

Growing up, I was a dedicated child of faith. I memorized long chapters of the Bible and even joined competitions to recite them from memory. But adulthood came with pain, and when I lost my father, my relationship with faith weakened. I had prayed for his healing, begged God to keep him alive, but He didn't. It broke me. For a long time, I felt forsaken.

Still, I wanted peace. I wanted to heal. And I could hear my father's voice in my mind *"when the world feels heavy, look unto the cross."*

That Thursday evening, I decided to go to church. I dressed up and went to a Faith Alive Church near my house. I got there by 4:00p.m., unsure when the service would start. The gate man said 5:00p.m., so I went in to wait.

Inside, I sat quietly, watching the cleaners dust the pulpit. Tears rolled down my cheeks. I felt like the prodigal child lost but yearning for home. I prayed silently for mercy and peace.

When the service began, I stayed through the one hour and thirty minutes of worship, prayer, and a short message about *living a life that pleases God.* I listened intently. Something in me felt still again.

After the service, I was the first to leave. Instead of taking a cab, I walked home. When I got to apartment, I saw missed calls from Chisom and Zainab. I returned Zainab's call first.

"Hal, sorry, I was sleeping when you called," she said softly. "These days I barely check my phone. Hope you're okay?"

"Yes, I'm fine. Just checking up on you."

"Oh, thank you. You know you can always come over, right?"

"I will, I promise," I said, smiling.

Moments after I ended the call, Chisom rang.

"What are you up to?" he asked.

"I just walked back from church. I want to shower and eat something."

"Church? That's new. How was it?"

"It went well. Just what I needed to lift my spirit."

"You good?"

"I'm fine," I said.

"Can I stop by?"

"Sure," I replied.

I regretted saying *sure* immediately. Chisom never visited empty-handed. True to form, when he arrived, he had enough food and snacks to feed an army.

"This would last for weeks," I teased. "Next time, don't bring anything."

We ate together, Speaking in hushed tones. across the kitchen counter. He asked if he could invite me to his church on Sunday. Normally, I'm picky about churches. Too many seem lost in noise and not the true gospel of salvation, however, I agreed.

# CHAPTER 13

I woke early, prepared masa mix; a northern delicacy and kept it aside for later. I told Chisom I'd fry it after church with cabbage sauce and chicken. He said he'd love to try it; the ones he's had before never impressed him.

He picked me up; we went to his church. It wasn't bad at all. The message was uplifting, the atmosphere calm. When they asked first-timers to stand, I didn't. I hate unnecessary attention. An usher kept glancing at me though, probably guessing I was new.

After the service, Chisom went to greet his parents. I noticed his mother looking in my direction, curious. When he came back, he said, "My mum asked about you. I told her I didn't want to make you uncomfortable, but she'll meet you soon."

"Thank you," I said quickly. "I'm not interested in meeting anyone's parents yet."

"Am I *anyone* now?" he asked, his tone soft but wounded.

"I didn't mean it that way."

"It's okay," he said quietly. "Just know I'm not playing about you. I really like you. I want to be with you."

Back home, I started frying the masa. Chisom stood beside me, curious.

"Can I try flipping one?"

"Sure," I smiled.

He seemed to enjoy it, and soon I was making cabbage chicken sauce while he handled the masa. Then, he accidentally splattered some batter on his shirt. Laughing, he excused himself to clean up. When he returned, his shirt was off, leaving only a white vest. His shoulders glistened under the kitchen light.

An unexpected wave of discomfort washed over me. Saleem would never be that casual in my home. I swallowed the thought. Chisom noticed my tension and said softly, "Sorry, I had to clean the stain. I left the shirt on the balcony."

We ate. He couldn't stop complimenting the food.

"My parents' anniversary is next week," he said. "I'd like you to come."

I hesitated but nodded.

"I'll always be by your side," he continued. "But if by next week you feel like you don't want to come, tell me. I won't insist."

When the day came, I made masa and chicken sauce as planned. Chisom picked me up. His family's house was beautiful but full of eyes. I felt their curiosity immediately. His father greeted me warmly, his mother more reserved at first.

Soon, his father was praising the masa. "Hallittah, this is great," he said.

Chisom's mother smiled faintly and said "Thank you. I asked the kids to store some Masa in the fridge for their father."

The conversation shifted to Nigeria's history, then the civil war. It made me uneasy, being a northerner and hearing about the atrocities committed on the Igbo's during the civil war. I was grateful when Chisom whispered for us to leave.

On the drive home, he smiled all through.

"You look happy," I said.

"My parents liked you," he grinned. "Makes marrying you easier."

"Marry me?" I laughed nervously.

"Yes," he said, in a serious tone. "If you'll have me."

When he dropped me off, he looked into my eyes. I wanted to look away but couldn't.

"I love you, Naima," he said.

I smiled faintly. "I'd be lying if I said I felt the same, not yet."

Still, I kissed his cheek before saying goodnight.

Days later, Zainab messaged that she was admitted to the hospital. I rushed over. She looked weak but insisted she was fine. Najeeb was there, exhausted but refusing to leave her side. I convinced him to go home and rest.

That night, Saleem walked in. My heart dropped. He brought a small gift basket and pancakes from our favourite café. He greeted us calmly, held Zainab's hand, he didn't say much, and walked out.

After he left, Zainab said softly, "I told Saleem you met someone. He met someone too, the girl seemed like a nice girl. You both need to move on."

I smiled faintly, but inside, I was breaking. I didn't know if the pain was from her words, or the thought of Saleem being with someone else.

When Zainab finally slept, I cried silently by her bedside.

By morning, Chisom came to pick me up.

"Are you okay?" he asked.

"I'm fine," I lied.

When I got home, I dropped to the floor and broke down. Chisom must have followed me in because suddenly, he was beside me, holding me as I wept.

When I calmed down, he helped me to my room. As he turned to leave, I whispered, "I love you."

He stopped, surprised, then smiled and kissed me gently. "I love you too," he said.

And for the first time in a long time, I didn't feel guilty for saying it.

Months passed and my relationship with Chisom grew stronger. I began to move on from Saleem. I focused more on work, and sometimes I wrote, but I also started to pray more. My faith deepened, and I found warmth and safety in Chisom.

One morning around 9:00a.m., I called him. He didn't pick up. I thought he must be busy. But when hours passed until 4: 00p.m.and I still hadn't heard from him, I grew worried. I called again by 5:00p.m., still no response. I thought of going to his office but held back. It was unlike him. I called Chiamaka to ask Miles if he had heard anything, but he hadn't. My chest tightened with worry; this was the first time he'd ever gone silent.

By past 8p.m., my phone finally rang. It was him.

"Hello, are you okay?" I asked, trying to sound calm.

"I'm so sorry," he said, his voice weary. "Please, I need you to understand I'm really sorry."

"What happened?" I asked quietly.

"I missed an email. One of our international partners and investors came into town unexpectedly. I got the reminder late last night, and so many things weren't ready. I had to work through the night with no sleep. I've been at the office all day trying to make things happen. These partners are the bedrock of our intelligence and security team."

I wanted to ask why he couldn't even send a text, but I swallowed it. He sounded exhausted. "Just go home and sleep," I told him softly. "You need your strength for the days ahead. And please drink some water."

"Thank you, my *Ima*," he said. "For understanding."

The truth is, I wasn't being understanding, I was simply saving the smoke for another day when his head could take it. I've learned that sometimes, we women let emotions speak louder than reason. I've taught myself to talk only when I can think clearly, so I won't regret my words later. To me, that's the truest form of femininity, asserting your point with grace, not emotion. I always try to reason, to first accord others the benefit of doubt. I give trust and sometimes try to put myself in their shoes. But I won't hesitate to walk away the moment someone tries to take my love for granted. That's what dating Jason taught me.

The following evening, around 5:00p.m., I got a call.

"Are you home?" Chisom asked.

"Yes," I said.

"I'm coming up."

Turns out, he was already parked outside my house. He came in holding flowers. I opened the door and let him in.

"Thank you," I said coolly, taking them.

"I know you're mad," he said.

"You scared me, Chisom. You could have at least texted; it wouldn't take a second. You just don't think I'm important enough."

"I'm so sorry," he said, sitting down. "I got carried away the moment I realized I was behind schedule. This was very important for the company. But you are important too. I can't even compare you to anything material, you're... essential. Please forgive me. What's a man without his livelihood?"

"It's fine," I sighed. "Next time, just text so I don't worry." He stood up and hugged me from behind. I handed him some oat-milk yoghurt while I quickly put a meal together as I could tell he was famished.

The next morning, I woke up to a text from Zainab: *"I've given birth."*

I screamed, danced around my room, and called her, but her line was switched off. I called Saleem.

"Hello, Hallittah," he said, his tone calm. "She's home, I know that's why you calling. Come over; we're all here."

"I'm on my way," I said, heart racing.

At Zainab's house, she sat surrounded by aunties and food coolers, looking tired but radiant. Her face lit up when she saw me.

"Come and meet your son," she said, smiling.

I walked through the women and peered into the bassinet. He was so tiny, his little hands reaching out.

"Congratulations," I whispered, hugging her.

"Hallittah, no one tells you how painful childbirth really is," she said, tears in her eyes. "This was pure pain. If I ever have another, my co-wife can take over!"

I laughed and held her. "You did it, Zainab. You brought life into this world. No one is bringing a Co wife into this house."

She smiled weakly. "Imagine after all this pain, the boy decides to look exactly like his father."

We all burst into laughter.

Holding her baby filled me with warmth. Watching her made me realize I wanted that too. Marriage. Family. My own child. I felt ready.

That evening, Chisom picked me up from Zainab's home.

"How did it go?" he asked.

"Beautiful. The baby's so cute."

"Do you want one?"

"Definitely," I said without hesitating.

When I turned and saw his grin, I knew he was being mischievous.

"Don't get any ideas," I warned.

He laughed. "Not what you think. I mean I'll give you a baby at the right time, in the right way."

Then he added, "I was thinking how about a trip to Bali next month?"

"Really?" I gasped.

"Yes. Our first vacation together."

"Oh my God, that would be amazing!" I said.

He smiled. "I've seen a few nice suites, some with double beddings."

I laughed. "Of course you have."

It's been five months since Chisom and I became official. We've kept our boundaries, showing intimacy in other ways. Sex has never been part of our discussions. Unlike me, who has never had sex except for that one time I almost gave in to Jason, Chisom has had his fair share of experience. But what makes me love him more is his respect for my values. That was my first rule before we started dating, sex is not negotiable. And he's never made me doubt his faithfulness.

Seven days after Zainab gave birth, the naming ceremony was held. When they shaved the baby's hair, I almost cried; it was a religious necessity in Islam. I'd grown attached to those soft curls. I sat on the mat beside her, surrounded by women, but part of me kept searching the crowd for Saleem.

Then I saw him seated near the entrance. Our eyes met. He smiled. I smiled back.

And in that instant, I felt it: that cold, creeping chill. Something was still there. Something deep and real. If life had not thrown its obstacles at us, if fate hadn't twisted our paths, I knew deep in my heart he would have been my life partner.

I was really looking forward to Bali. Chisom had told his parents about our plans, but I didn't tell my mum. Northern parents are wired differently. She knew I was dating, but in our culture and moral code, traveling with a man, one who hadn't married me, was simply unthinkable.

Whether Muslim or Christian, our northern parents share a similar lens. I already knew what she would say: *"A man who hasn't married you, and you're already traveling with him? He'll never take you seriously. He'll think you're an easy girl."*

I didn't want to hear that. As much as I respected her views, we thought differently. So, I saved both of us the argument. When I explained it to Chisom, he understood.

I told Chiamaka about the trip, and Zainab too, but I skipped the part about going *with* Chisom. I knew she would tell Saleem, and that was something I wasn't prepared for. So I simply said I was going to Bali for a vacation.

Chisom covered the entire trip, despite my offer to contribute he refused.

The journey from Abuja, Nigeria, to Bali, Indonesia, took about twenty-four hours, including stopovers. Just as the magazines described, Bali was a dream with lush green rice farms, bamboo huts, clear beaches, and fountains that seemed to breathe.

By the time we arrived at the resort, I was exhausted. The staff welcomed us in traditional skirts, offering chilled juice and bottled water. I drank two glasses of what tasted to me like freshly pressed apples.

CHAPTER

While Chisom handled the check-in, I admired the surroundings. The resort was small; it wasn't a five-star hotel, but it was intimate, beautiful, and worth every dollar of the $200 per night it cost. The rooms were made of bamboo and brick, a perfect blend of rustic and modern design, overlooking a rice field. The air smelled crisp, fresh and invigorating.

I hugged Chisom in gratitude, which led to a soft kiss. "Let's take a stroll after we rest," I said, and went in for a long, hot bath. By the time I came out, Chisom was already fast asleep.

When I woke up, hunger gnawed at me. He showered and we headed to the hotel dining area for dinner. The place was magical at night, the air cool, the lights soft, and the smell of food everywhere. We served ourselves at the buffet, sampling different soups, spices, and desserts. Chisom kept smiling more that evening than I'd seen him do in weeks.

As we walked back to the room, he stopped halfway, held my hands, and kissed my forehead.

"I'm glad I'm doing this with you," he said.

I smiled, melting into his embrace.

"You make me so happy, my *Ima*. I love you."

"I love you too," I whispered, resting my head on his lap.

"I want to spend my life with you if you'll let me."

"Of course," I replied. "I'm not dating you just to know you."

That night, we talked until dawn, our twin beds facing each other. Before we slept, he made sure the doors were locked and lowered my mosquito net, teasing, "We can't leave Nigeria without malaria and come back from Indonesia with it."

I laughed and fell asleep, eager for morning.

I woke to the sound of footsteps. Chisom was already up, heading to the bathroom. I begged to use it first. I was desperate to pee after all the juice I'd drank the day before. He laughed as I rushed in. When I came out, he leaned in for a kiss.

"Come on," he teased. "Morning breath kisses are part of life!"

I giggled and dodged him. "Not buying that!"

After showering, we met our tour guide, Mr. Lamini. He took us through the nearby town past colorful temples, and, to my surprise, a small church crowned with a wooden cross. He explained that Balinese Hinduism blended with

Buddhist and animist beliefs, something I have never heard before. We tried street food, bought trinkets, and wandered through markets.

Chisom bought me a pair of earrings and a soft, flowing dress. Later, we went to the beach. Coconut trees hung lazily over turquoise water. Chisom playfully dragged me into the waves, and we ended up soaked, laughing and enjoying the fresh coconut water.

When evening came, Chisom said, "Let's continue the tour tomorrow."

Back at the resort, I showered while he prepared for dinner. "What should I wear?" I asked.

"Anything you wear looks good," he said, then pointed at the milk-colored dress. "That one; it matches my linen shirt."

When we got outside, he held my hand. "I have a surprise for you."

He led me to the back of the resort, where red and white petals shaped a heart on the floor, encircled by candles and wine glasses. The sunset burned behind it all. Before I could make sense of any of it, he dropped to one knee.

"Will you marry me?"

I froze. My heart trembled. It was so private and intimate, just how I'd always wanted it. I knelt too, tears rolling down my cheeks.

"Yes," I whispered.

He stood and lifted me into his arms. I could barely speak.

Later, dinner was a feast of grilled seafood, fresh fruit, and shared laughter. Afterward, we wandered to the fire pit and roasted marshmallows. I showed him how to make s'mores with crackers and chocolate.

An elderly man walked by and smiled. "Congratulations," he said.

"Thank you," we chorused.

He stopped beside us. "You remind me of my wife," he said. "She loved these marshmallows too."

He sat down, sipping his tea, and began to tell us his story:

She was American, and he was Balinese. She came on vacation, stayed at the small resort he managed, and they fell in love. When she left, she promised to return and true to her word, she came back two weeks later. They got married, built this resort together, and ran it until she passed away five years ago. He smiled sadly. "She took a painkiller for a headache and never woke up. We never got the chance to have children... But this business is our child now."

We listened, moved by his story. That night, before we left, he introduced himself as *Mr. Kadek*, the resort owner.

Back in our room, I wrapped myself around Chisom. Desire stirred deeply between us. We kissed slowly, passionately until he pulled back.

"We promised to wait until marriage," he whispered.
And I was grateful he did...

But the next day, standing on the veranda at dawn, something in me shifted. The sky was soft and gray; the rice fields swayed gently. I turned to him and said, "Why can't we marry now?"

He looked stunned. "Are you serious?"

"Yes," I said. "Let's do it, just us."

At first, he laughed. Then, seeing my face, he realized I was serious.

Within hours, with Mr. Kadek's help, Chisom found a priest from the small church we'd seen the day before. The priest was delighted to officiate.

I wore the simple dress Chisom bought me in the market and a rose crown made by one of the resort staff. surrounded by strangers, we said our vows.

"May your sincerity and love blossom," the priest said. "And when faith becomes a cross, may you carry it with grace. I pronounce you husband and wife."

Tears streamed down my face as Chisom kissed me. We signed a handwritten certificate, which the priest promised to seal at the community center.

Later, Mr. Kadek hosted a small dinner in our honor. There were nine guests, most of them were unable to speak fluent English, but kindness needed no translation.

When everyone left, Mr. Kadek brought out a small box and handed it over to me. "This belonged to my wife," he said. "Since you're the first to marry here, I want you to have it."

Inside was a silver necklace with a delicate ring hanging from it.

"I bought her that ring in Idaho," he said. "She picked it herself."

I hugged him tightly, tears in my eyes. That night, Chisom and I prayed over the necklace before bed. I vowed to cherish it forever.

The next morning, I massaged Chisom's back with my shea butter and lavender oil. He did the same for me, we kissed passionately, our desires arose...

"Are you sure?" he whispered.

"Yes," I said, my voice trembling. "We're married now."

It was both pain and beauty, an awakening I would never forget. When it was over, I cried softly.

"Did I hurt you?" he asked, panicked.

"No," I said. "I'm just overwhelmed."

He bathed me tenderly, and in the morning fed me breakfast, and we fell asleep in each other's arms.

By the time we woke, it was almost evening. We took a long walk, hand in hand. "Someday," he said, "we'll come back here with our kids."

When it was finally time to leave Bali, we said goodbye to Mr. Kadek, who had grown dear to us. Chisom donated $5,000 to the small church where we got married, to help with repairs, and we promised to stay in touch.

As we drove away, I took off my head scarf, the wind brushed softly through my hair.

I looked down at the necklace Mr. Kadek gave me, the ring glimmering from the sunlight.

"It looks good on you," Chisom said.

I smiled. "It is a blessing."

The flight back home was quiet. It suddenly dawned on me; I was engaged and married. We exchanged soft glances and quiet kisses throughout the flight. When we finally got connected to the internet, Chisom began replying to emails just like the typical businessman that he is.

When we arrived in Nigeria, a car picked us up from the airport and drove us to his house. The car ride was silent, calm, yet filled with unspoken warmth. I began to see another side of Chisom: a more intimate, tender version of him that we hadn't explored before. He kissed my hand gently, drew me close to him.

When we got to his house, he lifted me onto his shoulders and carried me inside while his gateman brought in our bags.

"Stay with me for some time before we figure out the house arrangements," he said. "You're my wife now, and I don't want to waste time making it official here in Nigeria."

We agreed to keep the marriage a secret until after the traditional wedding. Not even our closest friends knew the full story. We decided to only talk about our *engagement* for now.

I called my mum and told her Chisom had proposed.

"Praise the Lord!" she screamed with joy. I could hear her singing, *'The Lord has done it! Finally, finally, finally!'*

She asked to speak to him.

"Hello, ma," Chisom said, taking the phone.

"My in-law! Congratulations! The Lord Almighty will keep you both. You've made me so happy. God bless you."

"Thank you, ma," he replied, smiling.

When I took back the phone, she said, "Hallittah, take care of yourself, okay?"

"Sure, Mummy."

Next, I called Chiamaka. She screamed so loud I had to pull the phone away from my ears.

"We have a wedding to plan! Chief bridesmaid loading!"

I laughed. "Who told you you'll be my chief bridesmaid?"

"Don't play with me," she teased. "Do you want a murder case?"

We both laughed. "Congratulations, girl," she said. "Honestly, I had a long day at work, but you just made it better."

Then I called Zainab to tell her I was back and would love to visit. Her voice sounded tired.

"Are you okay?" I asked.

"Yes, I'm fine. My baby's been sick, but he's doing better now. Just overwhelmed."

"I'll check on you tomorrow," I promised.

Chisom hugged me from behind, kissing my neck softly. "My wife," he whispered.

A smile spread across my face. "I'm a whole wife," I teased.

"Yes, you are. Now, I better pay your bride price soon. I'll finish my onboarding at work, and next month we'll start preparations to meet your family. I'd like us to visit my parents this Sunday, they knew I was proposing in Bali, and I'm sure they can't wait to hear everything."

I stayed over at his place. The next morning, Chisom dropped me off at Zainab's. I slipped off my ring because I didn't want my news to be a distraction.

When I got there, I found her sitting by her baby's crib, looking exhausted. She smiled weakly when she saw me.

"Don't mind me," she said. "He's so much better now. I have all the help I need; a nanny at night and another during the day, but I can't help but stay awake."

I rolled the baby's crib into the living room, tucked him in with his blanket, and told Zainab to lie down. One of the maids brought her an extra blanket.

"Just rest," I said. "I'll keep watch. Close your eyes; I'll handle everything."

She fell asleep within minutes. When the baby woke up, I picked him up, fed him, and rocked him gently in my arms. "Walk softly," I whispered to the house staff. "Let her sleep."

When Najeeb walked in and saw Zainab asleep, he looked at me and smiled quietly. "Thank you," he said softly. He lifted the baby from my arms. Just then, Zainab woke up.

"You're back," she said.

"Yes," he replied. "Just rest a little longer."

I urged her to sleep, but she insisted she'd had enough rest. She asked how my vacation went.

"It was beautiful," I said. "Nothing like I've ever seen."

She smiled. "I can't wait for my baby to be older so we can go on vacation too. Najeeb says we can go anytime, but I want him to be older. It'll be easier."

"Smart choice," I said.

I didn't tell her about my engagement. It didn't feel right at that moment. I promised to visit again the next day. Zainab asked her driver to take me home.

When I got to my apartment, the air was still and slightly dusty, the smell of absence. I opened the windows, swept the floor, wiped the tables, and threw my sheets into the washing machine. I texted Chisom to tell him I was home.

That evening, he came over with food, kissed me as he entered, and said, "Now I have two homes and so do you."

He offered to help. "If you can clean the kitchen counter again, I'll handle that," he said.

I took a shower, then joined him for dinner.

Halfway through, he looked at me and asked, "Who is Saleem?"

I almost choked. "An ex," I said quickly.

"You never mentioned him."

"Just like you've never mentioned yours," I said.

"True," he replied, smiling. "You only talked about that Jason guy."

I changed the topic, I don't like talking about my ex. Instead, I spoke about Zainab and her baby, then lit candles in the living room. I sprayed lavender mist on my sheets and stretched out the bed.

"You're such a woman," Chisom said, standing behind me. "It's hard not to fall in love with you."

"You've never told me why you love me," I teased.

He chuckled. "That's such a woman thing to ask."

"Maybe," I said, sitting on his lap. "But I'm asking."

He laughed. "First of all, it's everything the way you speak, the way you listen, how you talk about your father, your femininity. It's hard to explain, I love you because I'm made to love you."

Tears rolled down my cheeks. "I'm the luckiest girl in the world," I whispered.

He lifted me from the edge of the bed and laid me down in the middle. I snuggled into him.

"My *Ima*, if we continue like this, I might get you pregnant," he said playfully.

I nodded, smiling.

CHAPTER **15**

The next morning, I made breakfast. Chisom decided to go to work late so he could drop me off at Zainab's again. She looked much better this time, lively and bright.

"This is the Zainab I know," I said.

She laughed. "You remember when I traveled to Gombe? I told you I wanted to start a foundation focused on the girl child in the north. I'd love for you to be a board member."

I explained my vision of an NGO to address the cultural stigmas still limiting girls, even though more girls now attend schools. It would also strengthen the children's book club I'd already begun.

"So, do you want two separate foundations one for the girl child and one for the book club?" She asked.

"No," I said. "I'd rather have one that covers everything but focuses more on the girl child."

"Are you thinking of an English or Hausa name?"

"Whatever fits," I said.

"What about *Aminci Initiative*?" She suggested.

"I like that," she smiled. "*Aminci* means kindness."

We brainstormed a few more and finally settled on *Na Kowa Impact Foundation*. *Na Kowa* means "for all" in Hausa. It felt perfect.

"By the way," Zainab added, "Saleem is coming. Just giving you a heads-up. And what did you bring for me from Bali?" I laughed. "A nice dress, my bad I forgot it". I forgot it at Chisom's house, but I didn't want her to know that part yet.

She grabbed my purse jokingly. "Then I'll take whatever I find."

I laughed, but before I could react, she gasped.

"Hallittah… tell me this isn't what I think it is." She held up my engagement ring.

"Just say you walked into a store and bought this, and I'll believe you."

My face gave me away.

"Oh my God!" she screamed, jumping and dancing. "You're engaged!"

"Shhh, you'll wake the baby," I whispered, laughing.

"Tell me everything!"

"I wanted to tell you yesterday," I said, "but you weren't feeling well. I didn't want to be insensitive."

"Oh my God, Hallittah, I'm so happy for you!" she said, still dancing.

Just then, Saleem walked in. We froze. He'd seen the ring. My heart clenched it was too late to hide it.

He smiled softly. "Hey, monkey," he said to Zainab, then turned to me. "Hi, Hallittah. Congratulations, if it's what I think it is."

"Thank you," I said quietly.

"If you're wondering if it breaks my heart yes, it does. But I'm happy for you. Your ring looks beautiful."

He turned to Zainab. "Better collect your ring from her before she misplaces it. She lost the gold ring Najeeb got her during Musa's naming ceremony."

We all laughed awkwardly. He noticed the papers scattered around.

"What's all this?" he asked.

"A coup," Zainab said playfully.

"We're registering an NGO." I said

He nodded. "Keep the logo simple mature but sophisticated."

He ended up helping us finalize the logo and took on the task of registering the NGO. We spent the afternoon working, eating, and laughing just like old times. But I couldn't meet Saleem's eyes.

When Chisom came to pick me up, I felt relieved like I'd been holding my breath the entire time.

Later, Zainab called. "I noticed you were uneasy. Are you okay?"

"I'm fine," I said.

"And if you're wondering whether you hurt Saleem don't. He's fine. I believe he's moved on. Don't take it too hard, okay?"

"Okay,"

"And please, send my Bali gift before I storm your house."

"Yes, ma'am," I laughed.

Sunday came and we got ready to visit Chisom's parents. Prior to that day, his mum had called to ask for the ingredients I use in making masa, and I shared them with her. I promised to teach her how I make it, and honestly, I was looking forward to it. Still, I was slightly nervous. Chisom and I had just gotten engaged, and I knew it meant more attention on us.

When we got to his parents' house, Chisom squeezed my hand, an assurance that I would be fine. He led me through the door, walking right behind me. His mother, all glammed up, got up and drew me into a warm embrace, that felt unusual. I knew she had warmed up to me over time, but her reception today was even more welcoming.

"My daughter-in-law!" she said. "Congratulations to you, ohhh."

His father echoed the same congratulations.

"Finally, you've managed to hold him down. We had lost hope on him about marriage," Chisom's father teased.

Chisom laughed. "Lost hope? Come on, I'm barely in my 30s."

"No, you are an old man. At your age I had already had you and your sister," his dad replied, and everyone laughed.

"We are glad Hallittah has given you a reason to settle down," he added.

"Let us make the masa, because I want to show you two methods one, we can eat in an hour, and another we can fry tomorrow. You will choose the one you like more." I said

We all moved to the kitchen except for the men who remained in the living room. The white local rice had already been destoned, washed, and left to strain in a sieve. We used a glass blender that looked like the one my mum had years back in Gombe.

"This glass blender is old but strong," Madam Grace said proudly. "It's twenty years old. They don't make these types anymore, so I handle it with care."

"It really looks like my mum's own," I said.

"Oh really? How is your mum by the way?"

"She's doing great. I hope to visit her soon."

"That is good. Daughters should visit home often," she said with a soft sigh. "As you see, Chisom is the only one at home. My two other children are in the UK. They don't visit often, even my daughter. But I'll make an excuse for her because she calls me often. Daughters leave home, but their hearts are always home. Men are wired different, they focus on growth, the hustle. They remember home only when they get a nudge."

"True," I responded.

"But not my Chisom. He is different," she said with confidence and grace.

Even in the kitchen, Madam Grace carried herself with elegance. She wore loose kitchen gloves to protect her bright red nails.

We prepared the masa purée (blended rice). We kept a portion of the washed rice aside to cook because we were making two batches.

The first mixture was much softer and lighter. I added a semolina flour, some water, and the cooked rice while it was still hot. Once I made the mixture, I added the yeast, mixed it thoroughly, covered it tightly, and placed it inside the oven since it was the warmest spot for the yeast to activate.

Madam Grace wrote the whole masa process on a sheet of paper. "So I don't have to call you if I get stuck," she joked.

After an hour, I returned to the kitchen. We heated the masa fryer and began frying. Madam Grace brought out a chicken sauce she had prepared the previous day and kept in the fridge. She heated it, and we served everything together.

Chisom walked up to me. "I have been watching you from across the room. You're handling everything so well. Thank you for doing this for me... for us."

I smiled.

Chisom tickled me, I laughed.

"Share the funny story so we can all laugh!" his father said.

"It is a private joke," Chisom replied.

"You two are already showing your stinginess. Share the happiness!" his father teased. "By the way, Hallittah, thank you for sharing your masa recipe."

I smiled.

Chisom's mum brought out a box filled with head scarf.

"I noticed you tie your hair a lot. I got you some head scarf."

"Oh, wow thank you..."

I knelt halfway as a thank-you gesture and collected the box. I placed it on a stool and hugged her. She teared up immediately.

"Thank you, Hallittah," she said softly. "I am happy it is you he chose."

Her husband, noticing her emotional state, got up to hug her. My eyes welled up too. Chisom hugged his mum then came to wrap his arm around me.

"These women are trying to turn the evening into a crying party," his dad said, teasingly.

I saw the happiness in Chisom's eyes, and I knew I had made the right decision. At first, I was worried his parents might not accept me because they are Igbos from the Southeast region of Nigeria and I am Tangale from the Northern region, but that didn't even matter to them. Once they knew I was a Christian, that was I it took. It made me so happy. Deep down, I wish Nigerians could get to a point where we forget tribalism, honour our cultures, and still not allow them to divide us.

The evening at Chisom's home was beautiful. I heard so many stories of his mischief growing up as a child. We laughed and dined. When it was time to leave, he kissed me deeply once we got into the car, as though he'd been holding it in all day.

"I love you so much, my ímà. You have no idea. You are everything and more that I prayed for."

He kissed me again.

"I love my head scarf," I replied.

"But I love you more," I said, laughing.

"You're just silly," he teased.

After the evening with his parents, we drove back to his house and he asked, "So... for your birthday, what would you want?"

"Anything is fine."

"No, tell me."

"Well, I have always wanted to go to Bali you already made that happen. That was the ultimate birthday gift. I don't need anything else."

"Okay, how about a dinner with your friends? We could all go somewhere nice."

"You know I don't have many friends except Zainab, Saleem, some mutual friends of ours and Chiamaka who is now in Lagos.

I instantly regretted mentioning Saleem, but I kept it moving.

"Well then, invite them," Chisom said. "I'll make the reservations."

"Thank you," I said, and kissed him.

He smiled. "I like this type of thank you. Can I get more?"

I kissed him again.

"I need to marry you quick," he whispered.

As my birthday approached, I called Chiamaka. I told her my dilemma of whether to invite Saleem or not. I wanted to avoid awkwardness.

"Hallitah, if you truly have moved on from Saleem, inviting him shouldn't be a big deal. Above all, he is your friend. But if you have not moved on, please don't invite him. It depends on you."

"I have moved on," I said.

"Then what is the big deal?"

"You're right."

"You will miss my dinner, though," I reminded her.

"You will make it up to me," she said.

Even though I told Chisom I didn't want anything for my birthday, I woke up to a room filled with gifts from him and from his parents. He had also invited some of his friends, saying he wanted me to get to know "the boys."

I told Zainab to come with Najeeb. I sent an invitation to Saleem via text even though he didn't reply. I didn't want to ask Zainab about it.

When we got to the restaurant, I was shocked. The decorations, the flowers... I thought it would be a small dinner, but it was breathtaking and surprisingly, Chiamaka and Miles already seated.

"You said nothing about coming to Abuja!" I cried as she hugged me.

"We wanted to surprise you," she said.

Miles hugged me too. "We came all the way from Lagos to celebrate you."

Chisom introduced me to his friends. Then Zainab walked in with Najeeb carrying their baby, and right behind them was Saleem looking so good in his white kaftan.

I hugged Zainab.

"Happy birthday, baby girl! I wouldn't miss this," she said. "I dragged Najeeb and Saleem here oh!"

"I appreciate it," I said.

"Happy birthday, Hallittah," Najeeb said.

"Happy birthday, Hallittah," Saleem echoed.

Chisom came behind me. "Everyone, meet Chisom," I said.

Zainab smiled. "It is nice to finally meet you."

"You must be Zainab," he said.

"Yes, the one and only," she laughed.

"And this is Najeeb," I continued. They shook hands, Najeeb shook with the free hand since he was holding baby Musa.

"And this is Saleem," I said. They exchanged handshakes too.

CHAPTER 16

Chiamaka hugged Zainab excitedly. She greeted Najeeb and admired baby Musa, catching up like they hadn't seen each other in years.

Chisom suggested everyone grab plates from the buffet table. I had no idea it would be a buffet. There were different cuisines, varieties of meat, even suya. Chisom always went all out, especially when it involved the woman he loved.

Everyone was eating, but my heart was beating fast. Najeeb joined Chisom and his friends, while Zainab, Chiamaka, and I sat catching up. I noticed Miles and Saleem chatting too. I felt relieved no one was left alone. No awkwardness.

Later, Zainab's driver came with gift bags.

"The gifts are from me, Najeeb, and Saleem," she said. "I know you will know who gave what when you open them."

"I would be leaving soon. Happy birthday once again, Hallittah." Saleem said

"He means we will be leaving soon," Zainab corrected, side-eyeing him.

We said our goodbyes.

As they walked away, a wave of sadness hit me. I saw the sadness in Saleem's face too, though he masked it well. But I told myself he would be fine. Zainab had mentioned that he had a girl in his life.

Chisom walked up to me and I flinched.

"Are you okay?"

"I'm fine... just lost in thought."

"Care to share?"

"Nah, nothing deep."

"Okay... have you tried the peppered meat? It's so good," I changed the topic quickly.

"No."

"Come and have a taste," I said, pulling him to the buffet. We sat and I fed him.

Chiamaka came closer and teased, "Hmm, we go love oh!"

I laughed. "What is going on between you and Miles? You gave him more attention than you gave me."

She laughed.

"Spill it!"

"We will talk later," she said.

I turned to Chisom. "I knew it. These two are up to something."

He laughed and began choking lightly. I quickly handed him water.

"I'm sorry," I said.

He laughed. "Not your fault, the peppered meat was really spicy."

After everyone had left except Chiamaka and Miles, we packed everything into the car and drove to my house. We carried the gifts inside. I noticed a change in Chisom's mood when I kissed him goodnight, but I brushed it off. Maybe he was tired. He left with Miles.

As they drove off, I turned to Chiamaka.

"Now spit it out!" I demanded.

She laughed. "Alright, but first, let's open Saleem's gift. I'm curious."

"You read my mind," I said. "Let's do that, but you must tell me everything."

Inside Saleem's gift bag was a carved glass globe of a young girl wearing a head scarf she looked exactly like me, reading a book in a library by a window overlooking a huge garden. How did he get the girl to look like me? He once asked me what my dream life would be, and I told him... to have a family, a huge library, a garden view, and a peaceful place to write.

It was the best gift ever.

Inside the gift bag was also a book: *The Soul of Rumi*, translated by Coleman Barks. I cried even more. Carved at the bottom of the globe in tiny writing were the words: *Never forget you and the life you've always wanted.*

Chiamaka gently rubbed my back.

"I understand," she whispered. "You don't have to say anything. Instead of crying all night, let's drink tea and pamper ourselves with your magic herbal box. I'm flying back to Lagos tomorrow. Chisom flew us here just to celebrate you. I understand the bond you and Saleem share but look at the person you have a future with and forget Saleem. No sadness tonight it's still your birthday. Get me something to wear, let's start."

I wiped my tears, brought out the herbal box, and spread the mat I usually use for our skincare rituals. We spent the night pampering ourselves, laughing, unwinding ending the day softly.

The following day, Chisom and Miles came early to drop off Chiamaka's handbag so she could change her outfit. I made breakfast for all of us, and later we saw them off to the airport. Chisom drove. We said our goodbyes and left.

When we got back to my apartment, I went to use the restroom. By the time I returned, Chisom looked pissed. I asked what was wrong, and he said he had work issues he needed to fix. He said goodnight and left. His demeanour was off, but I assumed it was work-related. Knowing how seriously he takes his business, I brushed it off.

That night I called him. He simply said, "I'm busy, I'll call you back," and ended the call abruptly. My worry grew, but I tried to calm myself. The next day I called again to ask about work. He answered briefly, said he needed to concentrate, and that he'd call me back. His voice lacked love, it felt like he was speaking to a staff, not his lover. I felt irritated but told myself we would talk about it later. I decided I wouldn't call again unless he reached out.

Two days passed. Nothing.

I called and he didn't pick. Panic gripped me. I took a ride to his house since I had the spare key he gave me. He wasn't home. I left some of my belongings there and went back home. Another two days passed. Silence.

I felt unwanted, yet I needed answers. So I went to his office by 10:00A.M.

"Hey husband," I said teasingly.

He looked up and said he would call me later so we could talk in the evening that he was going through a lot and needed space.

His words pierced through me. A tear slipped from my eye. I left. I told myself that if he didn't call me that night, I would leave him for good. Because why would you hurt the one you claim to love?

That evening, I paced around my phone. He never called. I sat on the floor and cried.

The next morning, my mum called asking why I sounded sad. I lied that I was sick.

"Well, something terrible happened to Wasila," she said.

"Which Wasila?"

"The young girl in your reading club. She was raped by her neighbour."

"Jesus! What?"

"Yes. And her mother doesn't want to press charges."

"What? Why?!"

"She's scared for her daughter's future," my mum said. "The girl is receiving treatment."

"I'm coming to Gombe."

"No. Come when you're ready. Her parents want to keep the matter low."

I was furious. Mad. Everything in my life was crumbling, so I decided to travel home. I booked a car and arrived in

Gombe at night. I went straight to Wasila's house. She was asleep.

I asked her mother why she didn't drag the man to the police. She said she feared the stigma would destroy her daughter's future. When I insisted, we press charges, she knelt and begged me to let it go that the man had apologised and paid for treatment. She said if she reported it, her daughter might not get justice, and even if she did, "no one will marry her."

I was stunned. Angry. Heartbroken.

I asked if she wasn't worried the man would hurt someone else. She begged me again. My heart sank. What could I do if the parents refused to fight?

The next day I gathered the girls in my book club and had an intimate conversation about sexual abuse. Nine girls opened up about being touched by some perverted uncle, teacher, or cousin. Nine. I was shaken to my core.

Something had to be done.

I called Zainab and told her everything. She was furious too. We decided to take action. We convinced Wasila's parents to let us pursue justice in Abuja. Zainab used her family connections. The man was arrested at night and extradited to Abuja. He pled guilty and was convicted and sentenced to 15 years imprisonment.

Through the foundation, we raised awareness in schools, streets, and even gained an endorsement from the king in kaltungo my community. I drowned my heartbreak in activism encouraging parents and children to report abuse, ensuring offenders were jailed.

During the day I was fire. At night I cried myself to sleep.

I renovated my mother's house, trained men and women under the NGO, I created programs in multiple schools and ran book clubs. The work kept me alive.

After a month, I returned to Abuja. Before leaving, my mum asked about Chisom. I told her he was coming for introduction soon, I lied.

The same night I arrived; I went to his house. The cab driver waited outside. I opened the door and found Chisom sitting on the couch. My journal was beside him.

He looked up, then down.

"Who is Saleem?"

"Saleem is my ex."

"Is that not Zainab's brother?"

"Yes... but why are you asking?"

"Why did you keep that a secret?"

"Because it's in the past."

He sighed. "I saw this journal in Bali. I read some parts but assumed it was long over. But you are hiding him... and the way he kept looking at you on your birthday... the gifts... how do I know nothing is going on?"

"He is my past," I cried. "I love you."

He opened my journal and pointed to a page:

*Saleem gida ne*

*He is home*

*The comfort I feel in the North*

*He breathes ease and spreads it around.*

*My heart was meant for a love like that.*

My heart dropped.

"Yes, I loved him. But it is not who I am anymore. I never spoke about him because I didn't want to remember him. I chose you."

"I want to believe you," he said, "but it's hard. And that globe in your house don't tell me it wasn't from him."

"It is just a gift."

"You only opened his gift that night. You never opened ours. Everything together makes it hard to trust you."

"Chisom, I married you. Doesn't that count?"

"Thank God no one knew about that marriage. We can assume it never happened."

My heart shattered.

"Sex is just sex," he added.

That was when I stood up, dropped his key, grabbed my journal, and left. I sat in the cab and cried until no tears came. My head hurt. My soul hurt.

It felt unreal. Did I just give myself up for nothing?

Back in my apartment, I brought out the marriage certificate and wept. I wished death would come. The pain was unbearable.

My phone beeped. Zainab: "*Saleem is getting married.*"

I nearly died reading it. I cried out, begging God to kill me. I replied, "*I'm happy for him,*" but inside, I was dying.

I spent three days crying, barely drinking water. I knew I would die if I didn't gather myself.

So I ate what I could, hydrated, and eventually checked my phone. Chisom had messaged: *Can we meet and talk?*

I blocked him.

The only person my heart yearned for was Saleem, but I refused to be wicked. I wouldn't reach out to him when he was about to settle down. I couldn't tell Zainab either, because she would definitely tell him.

I wanted him to be happy.

So I packed my journal, flew to Lagos, took a cab past Badagry to the border, and entered into Benin Republic. The first time I came to Benin Republic, I followed my cousin who schooled there. I fell in love with the beaches.

I exchanged my Naira for CFA, I crossed the border, cleared at the Immigration and Port Health Authority, and found my way into Cotonou. I headed straight to the hotel I'd stayed in four years earlier. It looked newly renovated and aesthetically pleasing.

I paid for five nights.

The moment I got to my room, I crashed and cried again.

I am the chief president of running away from my problems, and honestly, I don't care as long as it helps me cope. I wasn't made to endure pain of any kind, so I will keep running, because I can afford to.

After wallowing in my sadness for hours, I finally got up and sat on the balcony chair. I let my mind travel with the breeze coming from the sea until sleep carried me away. The wind grew colder and woke me up. I showered and dragged myself to the outdoor sitting area. It was already dark.

I sat in the corner watching lovers laugh and giggle. Some white men with their Black wives and their adorable babies. *Maybe I should date a white man next,* I thought to myself.

Or maybe I should *join a monastery and become a nun or enlist in the army.*

I started crying again.

A man walked up to my space.

"Hello, can I take this seat?"

"Seat's taken," I said, not even looking at him.

"My bad," he replied and walked away.

I got up and stood by the railings, staring into the ocean.

*Maybe I can be a dolphin and swim away into the deep.*

My thoughts were becoming ridiculous.

I dragged my butt back to the room and slept.

When I woke up, hunger hit me like a slap. I hadn't eaten. Everything still felt like living hell. My heart wasn't fine, the hurt kept getting worse. I prayed out loud

> *"Dear God, forgive me for all my wrongs. Draw me close to You and wash me of this pain. It hurts. It hurts badly. Please help me?"*

To secure an uninterrupted week, I told my mother I was going to Benin Republic. She gave me her usual lecture about being a young woman and traveling so much, but I assured her that it was an important trip. I promised to phone when I returned, though secretly, I wished I didn't have to come back at all.

CHAPTER

I rushed downstairs for breakfast. My hair was a mess. I didn't realize how unkempt I looked until I saw my reflection on the breakfast tray. No wonder people were staring at me. I brushed my hair with my fingers and continued eating.

It dawned on me that if I continued like this, I might slowly run mad without knowing.

I went back to my room, bathed, combed my hair, tied a scarf, and wore a T-shirt with blue jeans. With my journal in hand, I went back to the outdoor seating area overlooking the ocean. Under an umbrella, I sat and penned my hurt exactly as I felt it. I cried while writing,

*The lack of been loved drives you crazy.*

*The memories of sacrifices laid bare on the altar of trust...*
*the gift of sincerity poured out freely...*
*You think to yourself, "This is it," not knowing it is only the*
*beginning of your foolishness.*
*A broken heart becomes your story.*
*Why does it always end badly?*

I put down my pen and closed the journal, its pages heavy with everything I couldn't say. Tears flowed until my eyes burned. Can tears dry up permanently if you cry enough? I wonder. Was I really wrong for not telling Chisom about Saleem? Did it matter that much? Yes, I loved Saleem but that was in the past. I flipped through my journal; it was true I had written more about him than anything else. But that is what an artist does she writes as her spirit moves.

I didn't want Chisom to know about Saleem. Not to hide him, but to bury him. I was afraid if I gave him a name in our present, I'd speak about him often.

So why did Chisom read my journal? That was the betrayal.

But was I wrong?

I sat there so long that a staff member finally approached to ask if I wanted water. I thanked him, my voice a rough whisper. As he walked away, a new sound cut through my haze.

"Hello?"

I jerked my head up, startled.

A man stood a few feet away, his posture cautious.

"My name is kelvin" he said. When I didn't respond, he gestures loosely toward the pool. "I was here earlier, swimming with my daughters, he paused, his eyes kind but concerned. "We went up for lunch, came back down and you're still here in the same spot. "I just wanted to check if you're alright."

I looked at him blankly, not realizing I was giving a dead expression until he stepped back politely.

"I'm sorry," I snapped back trying to fix my expression.

"Do you mind" he said pointing to the stool close to me and sat.

"Benin Republic is like a second home for us. My wife was from here; at some point we wanted to build a house because we come here often but she's late now. My girls and I still come every year to honour her memory."

"I'm sorry for your loss," I whispered.

"Thank you. Life happens." He said

"This is my second time in Benin. I live in Abuja. I needed an escape that didn't require a long flight."

One of his daughters ran up and tugged his hand.

"Daddy, you're taking long!"

"Say hi to this lovely woman!" he said

She hugged me, her finger still curled in her mouth. A sudden, unexpected warmth broke through the numbness in my chest.

"We're headed to the mall near the airport. You are welcome to join us." I offered a polite but firm decline. He nodded "well if you find yourself wanting some peace later, there's a place Called Dream Beach, not far from that mall. It's beautiful. We will stop there afterwards."

I went back to my room and took a nap, when I woke up, I decided to find the beach kelvin had suggested. After asking the receptionist for directions, she kindly summoned a taxi from the line outside that drove me to the beach.

I bought a giant caramelised double-beef burger, ate and layed under an umbrella I nearly slept, then I heard tiny footsteps approaching. It was Kelvin's daughter.

She screamed, "Daddy, I found her!" and ran off to fetch him.

Kelvin walked over, barefoot.

"How long have you been here?"

"A while."

"I'm glad you came out. Hope you like it here?"

I smiled. "I'm full. I just ate the biggest burger in Benin Republic."

He laughed.

We talked. About the vastness of Africa. About travel. About the elusive meaning of home. He spoke of his late wife. His youngest daughter Daisy dropped seashells into my palm before scampering back to the sand.

"Shall we walk a bit" Kelvin asked, nodding towards the water's edge. I agreed.

We walked in comfortable silence, pausing to watch the waves fold into themselves. My mind drifted far into the ocean. Tears escaped my eyes, tracing warm paths down my cheek.

"You'll be fine," kelvin said softly.

I didn't trust myself to speak.

"That's the thing about life "he continued "we go through things convinced it's our end, but it never is. Not as long as we're alive. And even in death, there is another form of life. Nothing truly ends."

He hugged me gently.

"You'll be fine."

We walked back. He rejoined his daughters to play. Later on, he offered me a ride back to the hotel, I accepted.

That night, I joined them for dinner. "Thank you for the company" kelvin said. I thanked him for his kindness.

When he invited me to go canoeing in Ouidah the next day, I agreed, I agreed without hesitation.

The following day was magical canoeing through a forest-like stretch of water, drinking fresh coconut water on the

Ouidah beach, eating the soft jelly-like coconut inside. I bought bracelets for kelvins daughters Daisy and Hannah.

I slept like a baby that night, when we got back to the hotel.

In the morning, I checked out and discovered Kelvin had paid all my bills. I asked the receptionist to call him. He came downstairs, we hugged, exchanged contacts, and I bid him farewell.

I crossed the border back into Nigeria and turned on my phone. Messages flooded in from Zainab, Chiamaka and Chisom.

I hissed and switched off the phone.

Of course he had reached out to my friends.

I went straight to the Lagos airport, bought a ticket, and flew back to Abuja.

I arrived in Abuja and took a cab home. The moment I stepped into my apartment, I paused. Something felt lived in. A slipper slightly out of place, the faint scent of someone else's cologne. Chisom. We had exchanged keys, and the last time we met, I forgot to take mine from him.

My phone came on, and his call flashed immediately. I stared at the screen, at his name glowing boldly, and pressed **block**.

Zainab called next.

"Haba, Hallittah! Do you want to give me a heart attack? Where have you been? I was worried sick!"

"I'm so sorry," I sighed. "I needed to clear my head, so I travelled."

"I understand. Where are you? Are you home? I'm coming now."

"It's late, Zainab. Let's meet tomorrow. I know why you're coming, and I don't want to talk about it tonight."

She exhaled. "Alright. See you tomorrow morning."

After the call, I quietly slid a key into the inside of the lock because if a key was inside, no other key could open it from outside. I felt Chisom might pass by.

Just as I suspected, someone tried to open the door later that night. The faint scrape of metal in the lock jolted my heart. I peeped through the window.

It was him.

I tiptoed back into my room, my chest tightening, heart pounding like it wanted to escape my ribs. I cried until sleep swallowed me.

Morning came harsh and bright. My head throbbed as though my skull had been used as a drum. I drank water and tried to steady myself, when a knock sounded. It was Zainab.

She hugged me tightly. "You know why I'm here. I don't support him at all. But Halli... he's been trying to reach you. He even called my husband. Apparently, they exchanged numbers on your birthday."

I blinked. "What? Why?"

"He saw what you wrote about Saleem and got jealous," she said carefully. "He said he acted stupidly. I explained your relationship with Saleem. But there's more."

I looked her concerned "what do you mean?" I asked.

"Saleem called off his wedding preparations. The lady Dinatu connected him with, he said he wasn't ready.

I sighed, "Zainab the betrayal hurts deeper than you think."

Before she could respond, my phone rang, it is Chiamaka.

"Girl! You scared me! I was going to call your mum, if I didn't hear from you this week. Hope you're, okay?

"Chisom called me, he said he wronged you, if you need an escape, come to Lagos."

"Thank you I am fine"

"I am glad you are "

I'll talk to you later." I replied.

After the call, Zainab held my hand. "When you're ready, please talk to him. He looks miserable."

She hugged me and left.

I called my mum to let her know I was back. I refused to read any message from Chisom. I didn't care what he had to say, cruelty has no space in my life.

But that night, Zainab called again.

"Please, Hallittah... just talk to him. You don't have to take him back. Just hear him out."

I sighed. "Fine."

I unblocked him and texted:

*Let's meet tomorrow. 9am. DanJos Café.*

I picked the café intentionally; it was the worst in the city. Their pancakes tasted like regret. It was a Perfect place for the conversation I needed to have.

And I chose working hours, because nothing mattered more to Chisom than work, he does not joke with work, I hoped he does not come.

I was disappointed when I got there.

He was already seated, dressed neatly in his corporate clothes. But when he lifted his head, his eyes were hollow. He looked like he hadn't slept in days.

"Hi, Ímá," he said gently.

I said nothing. I sat and waited.

"I'm sorry," he whispered. "I acted irrationally. I belittled you. I let jealousy blind me. Reading what you wrote about Saleem, broke me. I felt someone had loved you in ways I couldn't. But that's not an excuse. I'm sorry."

"I've forgiven you, Chisom. I spoke with no emotions, and I'm sorry for how I handled things with Saleem. We barely talk to each other; I should have told you he is Zainab's brother. But I didn't like talking about him."

"But I can't forget how you treated me," I continued. "How you called our marriage non-existent. Your words cut deeply. I've forgiven you, but I can't be with someone who is cruel."

I was unable to keep the straight face; I began to tear up.

He reached for my tears, but I stopped him. "Can I have my key back?"

"Ima... please"

I gave him his ring and placed it on the table.

"I took that marriage seriously Chisom. But now I have come to terms that it never happened."

I stood to leave. He held my hands then hugged me tightly. I didn't fight it. I cried into his shoulder, then pulled away and walked out.

Saleem called the moment I reached home.

"Can I see you?" he asked.

He came to my place, and we sat in his car.

"You look like you've been putting your eyelids through intense exercise," he teased. I laughed weakly.

He sighed. "Hallittah... if you love him, forgive him. He called me. Do you know what that means? A proud man swallowing ego to speak to his rival? He really cares."

I broke down.

"He called our marriage non-existent," I whispered.

Saleem froze. "Marriage? What marriage?"

"I got married to Chisom in Bali."

He softened instantly and wiped my tears. "Lover girl... you love deeply. I know. But don't let pain blind you from something real."

Saleem brought me food tuwon shinkafa with chicken kuka soup because he knew I wouldn't have eaten.

"Eat before I convince you to dump Chisom for me," he teased.

I laughed. I waved him goodbye as he drove off.

That night, I pampered myself with my honey hair mask, scrubs, oils, I am back to my rituals. I reclaimed my body from sorrow. My apartment smelled off warm rose and lavender. I felt human again.

When I heard a knock, I knew it is Chisom, I stayed quiet, when I later peeped through the window, he was sitting in his car. I have forgiven him, but I was just dragging it, besides he deserved it. A little shakara (attitude) won't hurt. When I opened the door, he stepped in, eyes red.

"My Ímá… I'm sorry. You are my wife. I am your husband. Please let it go"

I kissed him.

He lifted me onto the kitchen counter, breathless with longing and regret. We held each other.

I made him tea afterward. He showered, and wore my robe, it hung like a shirt on him. I massaged his feet as he exhaled deeply.

We held each other like lost pieces finally fitting again.

"We will visit my parents this week," he said softly. "I want to marry you immediately." I smiled.

CHAPTER

The next morning, I called my Mum. She was overjoyed to hear of the planned introduction.

I tied the grey head scarf his mum had given me for my birthday.

We stepped outside, hand in hand.

Chisom and I also drove to visit his parents. I remembered laughing. I saw a car drive into us.

*Metal screamed. Glass shattered. The world spun violently.*

"Ímá!" Chisom shouted, his voice fading into darkness.

When I opened my eyes, I was surrounded by metal and cold light. A doctor stood over me.

I tried to move.

I couldn't.

I tried to call Chisom.

No answer.

And that was when fear swallowed me whole.

"Where is Chisom?" I asked.

Someone touched my face.

"Mum? What are you doing here? Where is Chisom? What happened?"

My mum smiled weakly. "You had an accident. Chisom is fine. He's also admitted in the next room. You will see him soon. Just relax."

"Is he okay?"

"He's fine," she said, tears slipped from her eyes.

"But why are you crying?"

"I just feel sad that you're lying here like this. You've been unconscious for a while. You need to rest so you can get well."

"But why can't I stand up?"

"You will soon. Just lie down."

I tried to make sense of her words, but my head started to pound. I squinted and told my mum. She pressed the button for the doctor. I complained about the headache, about my body not moving. Tears flowed freely. I felt pain.

The doctor asked me to close my eyes and stay still. I don't remember what happened next.

I just drifted away.

Later, I felt a familiar hand holding mine. Chisom. He looked perfect, as if he had never been in an accident.

"You look better than me," I said.

"My head hurts. My body hurts. I can't move."

"You will be fine," he whispered. "I just healed up quicker."

I was relieved. As long as he was okay, I could endure anything.

I blinked, and suddenly he wasn't there.

"Chisom?"

No answer.

My mum stood at the door with her big black Bible.

"Mum, where is he? He was just here."

She excused herself and stepped out. When she returned, Zainab, Chiamaka, and Saleem followed behind her.

"You all look sad," I said. "But I'll be fine. I'll get better. They've tied me with chains."

They laughed nervously.

Chiamaka came closer. "Where is Chisom" I asked, "I just saw him"

"You probably had a dream. You have been sleeping." Chiamaka said

"I want to see him. Is he awake? Did he ask of me?"

The doctor entered with my mum.

"Can I go to him?"

"We can't move your bed yet," the doctor said gently. "Same with Chisom. You both need rest."

"Can I speak to him on the phone?"

I don't remember their response. Everything became heavy again. My tongue, my eyes, even my breath felt pinned down. The world blurred, and I fell asleep.

When I woke, things felt different. Their clothes were different. The air felt different. It looked as though time had passed. I was sinking into a body that refused to respond. They told me to rest; to heal quickly so I could leave the hospital.

They removed the catheter, unscrewed metal braces from my body, strapped a back brace around me. I couldn't stand, but I could finally sit if supported, but not for long.

My mum looked at me and began to cry even though I was improving.

"Mum, I'm getting better. Why are you crying?" I asked

She wiped her eyes. "I need you to understand something. When I heard about the accident, I rushed down from Gombe. You and Chisom were both admitted in this room. He had terrible injuries to his head and back, but he wasn't unconscious like you. He held your hand sometimes. He asked us to push his bed close to yours. But his legs his legs were badly wounded."

She paused, swallowing a sob.

"He went into shock several times. They moved him into the critical unit. A day before you woke up, he passed."

My world shattered.

I felt my soul collapse inside my chest.

Everything became a ringing silence.

I passed out and was eventually induced into a coma to protect my brain and heart.

When I woke up, the heaviness had returned. The pain in my chest was like a caught between my ribs, swelling until it felt as though it was choking me from the inside.

I begged to see him.

My mum spoke with the doctors. His parents agreed.

They wheeled me to a cold room. The mortuary. Chisom lay on a metal table, pale and still, utterly unreachable. They lowered the table so I could touch him. His skin was ice, pale and unyielding.

I held his hand, touched his face.

"I will love you forever."

I pressed my upper body over him, crying, and for a fleeting moment, I swore I felt him move.

They pulled me away gently. My body was shutting down again. Everything went dark.

When I woke again, Chisom's father was sitting beside my mum.

"Even when you are supposed to look horrible," he said softly, "you still look pretty."

I smiled. His humor always reminded me of Chisom.

He came closer. "Don't worry too much. He has gone to a better place a place where busy Igbo men finally learn to rest."

He wiped a tear.

"We are grateful he brought us a beautiful woman like you. We love you. Heal for us. Heal for your mum."

I cried until I could not breathe.

I stayed in the hospital for a month. Every day, I begged to go home. When the day finally came, I requested to stop by the morgue one more time. I touched his chest, left the scarf he loved by his side, and whispered, "Thank you for loving me."

They closed his coffin.

Najeeb arranged a private jet to fly his parents and his body to Imo state for the burial. I was not allowed to go because of Tradition.

I was going through immense pain and grief.

On our way back I realized we were driving somewhere other than my house. I asked why and Zainab answered, "You can't use the stairs yet; we are taking you somewhere accessible."

The new house was arranged with great details. I smiled in appreciation.

My books were arranged on a low shelf, so I can have easy access.

My brother and cousin were there to help lift me. My mum helped me settled in. The nurse was waiting with IVs I didn't want but needed. I hate needles, but I had no strength to argue.

I found out later the nurse probably induced sleep so I wouldn't break myself mentally.

That night, in my new room, with my back braces, my pain, and my swollen eyes, all I could think was:

*How can love die when the body that carried it is cold?*

*And how can I live when my body still remembers his touch?*

I woke up angry the next morning. Not at anyone in particular, just angry at everything: at my body, at my helplessness, at the fact that I couldn't even decide when to sleep or wake. It felt like I was no longer in control of my own life.

"Mum," I asked quietly, "why am I always being induced to sleep?"

She looked at me, surprised. "I don't know, Naima. The doctors gave the prescriptions. I think it is meant to help you rest. If you stress yourself, it could affect your healing. I know you're tired, but everything we're doing is for your own good."

I knew she was right. And I knew she was just as drained as I was.

"I just want to stand," I whispered.

"You will," she said. "The doctor will tell us when you can start physiotherapy."

I said a silent prayer *God, please speed up my healing.*

I visited Chisom's parents when they returned, but the moment I saw his mother's face, I broke. Every visit became a flood of tears. I needed to see them, yet I also needed distance. It was a painful balance.

My mum set me up in the living room, surrounding me with pillows to support my back. I stared at my body, the braces, the scars, the bandages and wondered how my life had changed so completely.

I didn't know what my future looked like anymore.

I didn't know when I would walk again.

I didn't know what to feel.

A tear fell. Then another.

A knock came. My mum opened the door, it was Zainab and Saleem.

"Hey pretty," Zainab said, smiling softly.

Saleem stepped forward. "Hi, Hallittah. How do you feel? Better, I hope. You look better."

"Thank you."

Zainab handed me the phone. "Chiamaka wants to speak to you."

The moment I heard her voice, tears poured out all over again.

"You sound better," she said. "I'm praying for you."

"Thank you. You stayed with me for a whole week, and I didn't even call... I'm sorry."

"Oh, please," she replied. "You're the strongest woman I know."

We ended the call. I felt lighter and heavier at the same time.

We talked for a while, but their conversation felt filtered. Too careful. Too soft.

"You guys are terrible," I finally said. "You can't even gist properly because you think I'll be jealous of life outside. Give me the real gist!"

They burst into laughter.

"Fine," Saleem said. "But I promise you're not missing anything outside."

A sharp pain shot through my back. My mum rushed forward, transferring me gently from the couch to my wheelchair, then to my bed. Zainab covered my legs. Saleem stood by the pillar, watching me with a pity he couldn't hide.

"We'll see you tomorrow," Zainab said, squeezing my hand.

After they left, my mum sat on the stool beside my bed.

"I noticed how Saleem looks at you," she said quietly.

"Mum!!!"

"I'm not suggesting anything," she continued. "But you two must be very close."

"Yes. We're good friends."

"When you were unconscious Chisom told Saleem 'to take care of you."

I froze.

"What!?"

"He said it. Zainab, Chiamaka, and another young man were in the room, but he only spoke to Saleem."

My chest tightened.

"Mum, are you sure?"

"I am" she continued. "Sometimes, when a person loves you deeply, they want to make sure you have someone trustworthy beside you, when they're not around anymore."

I looked at her, feeling confused, hurt, grateful and overwhelmed.

"And Saleem's family are the ones who found this apartment for you. They moved your things. They made it comfortable. They also paid your hospital bills."

My eyes widened.

"Mum, why didn't you tell me?"

"I planned to. You can thank them tomorrow."

"I'm really lucky to have them. They're family."

## CHAPTER 19

The next morning, Zainab and Saleem came with my favourite pancakes.

I was on bed rest, as the nurse suggested; she said I needed to show "extraordinary progress" before the next hospital check-up.

I thanked them for their help. Zainab hugged me gently.

"You're family," Saleem said. "You're allowed to get tired of us, but we're not going anywhere."

"How is baby Musa?" I asked

"He is growing real fast"

"The biggest betrayal of my life? Musa's first word was 'Dada'. He won't say 'Mama'! He even mumbles *Uncle Saleem* but ignores me. If Hallittah lived with us, he'd probably call her name first!"

We laughed.

My mum walked in after taking a phone call.

"Chisom's dad is coming," she said.

"Why "I asked

"He said it has to do with some paperwork"

Later that day, he arrived with a lawyer.

"Hello beautiful," he said softly. "I Came to see you with Chisom's lawyer."

"Why is anything wrong...?" I asked with concern.

"You're his next of kin," the lawyer said. "Chisom made changes months ago."

I was shocked. when I saw the dates he'd made the changes, it was a week after Bali.

The same week he told me the marriage meant nothing to him, the same week he stopped talking to me because of Saleem.

And yet he updated his will. I began crying uncontrollably. Only Saleem knew we were married.

The lawyer tried to explain Chisom's will, but I shook my head. "I don't want anything. Give everything to his parents."

"You don't have to decide now," The lawyer insisted.

"I don't want it," I repeated.

Zainab rubbed my hand gently. "Calm down," she whispered.

Chisom's father spoke softly. "Take your time my dear, we are not contesting, it was his wish."

When everyone stepped out, Saleem remained. He sat on the edge of my bed.

"Chisom loved you deeply," Saleem said. "He was serious about everything."

"I feel so bad, for doubting him. When he said the marriage meant nothing, I thought he meant it ... but he really loved me. However, I can't take anything from him."

"Do what you feel is right," he said.

So, when we met again with Chisom's family and lawyer, I signed the document, returning everything to his parents.

"I am the luckiest woman alive... to have been loved by him. To have known a soul so intentional," I told them. I would carry his love for the rest of my life.

Weeks passed. I realized I could move my neck freely and sit upright for longer. Something in me awakened. I had hope. I began reading again. Most evenings, I spent with Saleem, who had slowly turned my living room into a workplace.

One day, he caught me staring at him.

"Don't judge me," he said, smiling. "I'm here by my free will and Chisom's. He told me to take care of you. You can ask anyone who was there. Besides, what other work do I have? You're stuck with me."

Surprisingly, he and my mum became friends in no time. She always made kunun zaki, a northern Nigerian drink made from millet, dried sweet potatoes, and rice seedlings. He loved it. She made sure the fridge was always stocked, and when it was time to pray, he would simply choose a corner and pray.

There were days I chased him away. I even pretended to be angry, so he'd leave. But he only smiled and looked me in the eyes.

"You can't get rid of me," he said softly. "I promise I'll leave when you start walking."

The doctor said I needed several more months to heal before physiotherapy could begin. The news shattered me, but I was determined. It wouldn't be long before I could stand again.

One morning, I woke to find over ₦40 million in my bank account. Shocked, I showed my mum, then asked Saleem who was eating in the living room if he had anything to do with the deposit.

It wasn't until Chisom's father called that I understood.

"I know you said you didn't want anything," he said. "This is just a small token from Chisom's account. Please don't refuse it. Use it as a safety net, whenever you need."

I thanked him, my voice unsteady and ended the call.

Some mornings were joyful. Other days were terrible. I felt bad that everyone had to deal with my mood swings. Some days, I wished I could be alone so no one would suffer from my actions... But every time I snapped, all I got in return was patience, smiles, and soft apologies. Even their kindness frustrated me.

Everyone was at my beck and call. I was grateful but sometimes the gratitude suffocated me.

Eventually, I insisted on seeing the doctor, I wanted to share my frustrations and get an approval to begin physical therapy.

"Hallitah," he said gently, "you are strong. Your frustrations are normal. You take pills, you stay in one position for long it is understandable. Physically, you've healed greatly. You can begin physical therapy. But I would also suggest emotional therapy. I will connect you with someone. Talk to her. Let your frustrations out."

The therapist came to my home to ease my movement. She was kind and soft-spoken, but her presence irritated me. Opening up to a stranger felt stupid.

"Hallitah," she said, "what do you think about therapy?" "Not much," I replied. "I've never had to do this, and the only time I hear about therapists is in books. I don't even believe Nigerians go for therapy."

"I understand what you mean" she said

"You don't sound Nigerian at all and that proves my point" I said.

"I am Nigerian" she said. "And yes, most people don't believe in therapy, but I assure you, it has helped many. I hope it helps you too." "How do you feel?"

"Terrible," I replied.

She looked at me calmly. "You seem to be handling things well. I won't push this session. Today, let's just get to know each other. Be kind to yourself, that is the most important step. Everything will fall in place. You will find joy again."

She was about to leave when Saleem and Zainab walked in with baby Musa. The sight of him made me smile. I hadn't seen him in a while. He was growing into a handsome, bubbly little boy with the cutest giggles.

"How did it go?" Saleem asked.

"Okay, I guess."

He laughed. "You hated it, right?"

"Yes," I smiled.

"I knew it," he teased.

Zainab rolled her eyes. "Are you encouraging her to chase away her therapist?"

"That's not what I said," he protested.

They looked cute anytime they go at each other

"What's in the paper bag?" I interrupted their banter. "Because I smell pancakes, and I want mine hot."

They laughed.

"Well, welcome back," Zainab said. "Funny Hallittah is finally popping up."

She served the pancakes, and I shared mine with baby Musa, who was clearly showing signs he is going to be a foodie like his mum.

"He doesn't look like you," I teased Zainab, "but he definitely has your appetite."

Saleem laughed. Zainab rolled her eyes at him.

Zainab went into the kitchen,

"You are doing great, Hallittah," he said.

I smiled but began to cry".

"I wish I could take your pain," he whispered. "I hate seeing you sad."

I couldn't even explain why I am crying. These days I cried for everything: for my body, for my losses, for the weight of being alive.

Zainab returned with bottles of *kunun zaki*. She noticed the change in the room.

"Are we crying?" she asked. "So, I can join?"

Her words made me laugh. Even baby Musa smiled.

The physiotherapist Finally came the following day, I was happy and eager to begin. After examining me, he put a back brace on me and started moving my legs and arms. The stretching felt relaxing until he held me upright with the support poles.

A sharp pain shot through my back. I nearly peed on myself.

My joy shattered into tears.

"It won't be easy," he said calmly, "but with determination, you will make progress. For now, I'm just finding strength in your limbs. Later we'll work on your core and back. There will be pain, but I promise it won't be unbearable."

The eagerness disappeared; I didn't want to continue. Fear shook me. I felt dizzy.

To calm me, he massaged my feet with some minty oil. His hands worked gently on my body I was a bit uncomfortable, but it felt great. My mum's presence eased my discomfort. Since I didn't need to undress, I relaxed and enjoyed the massage.

Soon afterwards I dozed off.

When I woke, I felt lighter almost like I could walk.

I was already looking forward to his next visit.

When Saleem came that evening, I told him everything that happened.

"So," I asked cautiously, "what happened to the lady you were supposed to marry?"

He was silent for a moment.

"I didn't want to hurt her," he said.

"You can't hurt anyone, you are not capable of that," I said.

He smiled. "Not physically. Emotionally. I felt I wouldn't be able to love her when I still love someone else. It wouldn't be fair."

I understood immediately and retreated.

"I'm sorry if I was too direct," he apologised.

I shook my head, unable to speak.

Guilt washed over me guilt for ruining his life, for even having this conversation when Chisom had given me everything, for feeling something I shouldn't feel. Even for being alive.

"You deserve love, Saleem," I whispered.

"My heart is open," he said softly. "I'm just waiting for love to choose me back."

"Silly. Trying to be poetic I see?"

"My poetic partner in crime," he teased.

I noticed my mum smiling from the corner. When our eyes met, she quietly walked away.

"I can't wait to walk," I told him.

"You *will* walk. And when you do, we'll travel to Konya."

"To visit Rumi's tomb? And buy as many books as you want," he said.

"That sounds like it is going to take forever."

"Do you believe it will take long?" Saleem asked

"No."

"Then hold onto that faith." He said

I smiled. Then guilt crushed me again. Chisom was barely buried, and here I was, dreaming of Turkey with another man.

A wave of sadness hit me.

Saleem noticed.

"I believe Chisom would be happy that you're happy," he said quietly. "He put me in charge of your smile. You can be sad, and that's okay. I just don't want you to be sad for too long."

Life began to look hopeful again not because I could walk, but because I was tired of being negative. Since I couldn't die now, I had no choice but to start doing the things that made me happy. I began tying my head scarf the way I used to, I wore a floral dress that day and finally put on perfume.

I looked forward to my physiotherapy sessions every time. And I eventually fired my therapist. She was good, but I honestly didn't need her. I told the doctor politely that I was fine. He insisted at first, but I promised him I had improved greatly. Besides, he could see I no longer came to the hospital in pyjamas and sweatpants my small revival convinced him. I looked happier.

I wrote as much as I could. I read countless books. And the more I read, the stronger the feeling grew that maybe, just maybe, I could become a great writer. Maybe this was my chance to learn the art of writing.

Saleem bought me so many jotters and journals.

"Write your heart," he said. "And I promise never to read any of it without your permission."

Before I knew it, a year had passed.

I still couldn't walk. But the doctor encouraged me to remain hopeful.

I had started wheeling myself around the house. Saleem bought four new wheelchairs, two of which was imported from the UK. He had become my closest companion. Though baby Musa might disagree; he seemed to love my company even more, especially when he rode around on my wheelchair like it was his own personal amusement park.

With time and therapy, I could finally take myself to the restroom. I was beginning to get some privacy though my mum always stood by the bathroom door. A chair was placed inside the bathroom so I could use it to seat and shower safely. Some days I couldn't reach my feet, so my mum knelt and washed them for me. Especially on days I did physical therapy, I will get so tired.

# CHAPTER 20

O ne morning, I woke up terribly sick and before I knew it, I was rushed to the hospital. I prayed to be well, for my mother and for Saleem, who looked deeply troubled.

It turned out to be a high fever.

When I got back home, I asked to be taken to a park so I could sit under a tree. My mum was worried at first, but Saleem assured her I would be fine. He carried me into the car, and we picked up Zainab and baby Musa. We strolled through Kanji Park. I just needed fresh air. I was becoming depressed indoors, and the outing worked. In the evening, Saleem brought me home, wheeled me inside, and went back to his house.

But my worries had shifted; now I was worried for Saleem. It felt as though I'd trapped him. So, the next morning, in front of Zainab, I broke down crying.

"Please, Saleem," I begged, "go live your life. You've taken care of me enough. I'm holding you back."

He looked at me for a long moment, his voice firm and soft at the same time.

"Hallitah," he said, "I broke off my relationship with Aisha long before any of this. By then I was sure you would get married, I made peace with that. I did it when I realised, I couldn't love her while loving someone else. This has nothing to do with you holding me back. This is about what *I* want. Being here takes nothing from me. I go to work, and when I'm free, I come here. This is the life I choose. Don't push me away because of what you think. I am a grown man with a choice."

He swallowed, his voice trembling slightly, but steady.
"I truly care for you. I love you."

My heart started beating fast.

"I asked you to marry me in the past," he continued, "and we both agreed it wasn't possible. But don't push me away this time. That request is still on the table. I wish you could see that everything I feel for you is genuine."

"Wow," Zainab blurted out, then stormed out of the room.

Saleem didn't stop.

"I love you, Hallittah. I don't want to be pushy, but I've found companionship and friendship in you, something I've never felt before. Even if you won't marry me, don't push me away.

If you insist, I will go, so you don't feel like I'm suffocating you. But I *want* to be here."

Something in his eyes was different fearless, intense and honest.

I looked away, and my mum who had quietly stood in the corner began crying. She walked into the kitchen.

Saleem held my hand gently. "Don't do this to us," he whispered.

Then he stood up and stepped outside the house.

I was completely perplexed. Did I love him? Yes. Did I feel guilty? Yes. But even if I wanted to be with him not in this state. Not when I still felt broken.

When Zainab and Saleem came back inside, her eyes were swollen. She walked straight to me and hugged me tightly.

"Marriage and motherhood have turned you into a softy," I teased.

She smiled.

"You idiot! Can't you let this emotional moment last?"

I laughed.

"I love you, Hallittah," she said. "You're like my own blood sister. You idiots have made me more emotional than my own love life. If you two don't end up together, I will sue you both for emotional distress."

We laughed.

My mum walked out with a small nylon bag.

"Saleem," she said, "I packed some kunun zaki for you. Share with Zainab."

They thanked her and left.

After they were gone, I turned to my mum, "Are you okay?" I asked.

She looked at me, thoughtful and calm.

"If you're asking because you want to know how I feel about Saleem that I cannot decide for you. He is a great man. He genuinely loves you. I don't know your full history, but I see how he treats you."

She sighed and continued,

"The Bible is clear about being equally yoked with unbelievers. I didn't write it. If you asked me strictly as a Christian mother, I would tell you not to marry him. But if I'm being honest with this the facts the sacrifice and love he has shown you, he is more capable of loving you than many Christian brothers I have seen. I have never seen a young man this patient."

She paused, her voice softening.

"He has a great light in him. If it is kindness and home training, he has it in abundance. I would sleep in peace knowing you are with him more than with any other man. I never believed I would say this, but I will not say no to whatever you decide."

I smiled.

My mother is a devout Christian. She has never approved of inter-religious marriages. Her response shocked me.

But I felt hopeful.

The following morning, I heard a knock. I was seated on the couch facing the door. I knew it was Saleem, he let himself in just like he always does. He knows the door is never locked. He came in with a bright smile when he noticed I was there.

"I just know you are the person,"

"Is it because of my signature scent?" he asked

"No, I know you will walk in after knocking, I think we should just make room for you in this house,"

"That would be awesome. But we can do that when you agree to marry me."

"Where is your mum?". he asked

"Probably in the kitchen or lying down in her room."

"You look like you're coming from work."

"Yes, I am always working. You know I work two jobs, right? I work for my dad's company and also abroad. So, I am juggling both. I've been contemplating leaving the work abroad, but it keeps me grounded. Even though my dad's work pays me more, I use the UK company work as an excuse to escape my dad's grip otherwise, I might not have a life of my own."

"Oh, I didn't realize just how hectic it is for you."

"Actually, it's not that hectic. I have tried leaving the UK company, but they just won't let me go. They made work flexible, so I can be here in Nigeria and still execute projects and meet deadlines."

"I miss working," I said.

"I know. You don't have to worry about that. You can focus on anything that would make your life easier, and we would do the work for you." I smiled

"Saleem, why do you want to marry me?" I asked

"Firstly, I hate going back to my apartment when I come to see you. And I want to experience the herbal concoction and treatments you, Zainab, and Chiamaka enjoy," he said. I laughed.

"Above all, you make love easier. Even when we are quiet in the house and not saying anything, it feels electrifying. I can say many things, but I think it's just a 'you effect'. I can't put it into words. Sometimes you love someone and can't pinpoint one thing exactly that you love about them— because it is everything: your presence, your aura, It's you."

It is one thing to be mesmerized by words, but it is a whole new game when it is backed up by actions. That is who Saleem is.

When Saleem left that day, Zainab called.

"Do you know Saleem told Hajiya and Baba that he wants to marry you?" she blurted.

"What do you mean?" I asked.

"What I just said! Saleem told them."

Hajiya called to ask how you were doing, and I said you were doing a lot better.

"Oh, wow," I exclaimed.

That afternoon when I told my mum that I wanted to be with Saleem she said "The ball is in your court. I am here for you, with or without Saleem. It is my responsibility as your mother to be here for you until death do us part."

My mum has been with me since the accident. It has been more than a year, and I know she misses her home. I really want her to take a break, but she insists on staying back. I have all the money and support I need to be fine, but she chose not to leave me for someone else to take care of me.

I am still trying to put together a list of what I can do with my life, and every time I try to think about it, I go into depression. When I heard a knock on the door, I knew it was Saleem. He walked in and came to the table where I had my pen and paper scattered.

Someone looked pissed.

"How can I help?" he asked.

"Help me figure out how to be useful," I said.

"Let us take a walk," he suggested.

He pushed the wheelchair as we got out, we got to a tree, and he sat on a stone. "It is always great to be outside," I said.

"I knew this would cheer you up."

Tell me something you'd love to do," Saleem asked.

"It is vain, but a core fantasy of mine "

"What is it?"

"Dancing. Sometimes I imagine myself in a place like Verona, or any beautiful town in Italy, holding someone I love and swaying to a jazz song. It would be even more perfect if it was raining, and we were dancing with a beautiful view."

"I have a great idea," said Saleem.

I turned and looked at him. "We could do that in Ibadan."

I laughed hard. The sheer absurdity of comparing the ancient, rust-roofed sprawl of Ibadan to the romantic postcard of Verona was what sent me over the edge.

He continued, "Don't laugh, listen," he insisted. "We could do that, then have tea while dancing. The next day, we go and find a 'mama put' restaurant and have a hot bowl of amala and ewedu soup."

A fresh wave of laughter seized me, this time so intense that tears began to stream from my eyes.

He looked at me, his expression softening into something earnest and profound. "Just say you'll marry me, Hallittah."

I looked at him and said, "I will marry you, Saleem."

He looked stunned. "Please don't joke about this."

"I am serious," I nodded.

"You are going to make a grown man cry, in public, do you mean it" he asked

"I do "he kissed my hands.

"Whew. Finally."

He wheeled me back home, and we sat outside the house.

"The first thing we will do when we get married is travel to Konya, Turkey, to Rumi's tomb and the surrounding libraries. Then we will end up in Verona, Italy, before coming back home. I have been planning this trip, to surprise you.

looking for wheelchair-accessible places. Now we get to do it together."

Nobody objected to the wedding not even Saleem's parents. My mum didn't say much and told my father's brother to accept my dowry as customs permit and not say a word. We had a court wedding and refused a flamboyant celebration because I was not comfortable with it, and Saleem wasn't down for it either. It was a quiet get-together and dinner, which I was absent from toward the end because sitting for too long made my back hurt. I begged Saleem to stay back. But he later joined me inside.

"I was beginning to worry that your back might be hurting," he said. I was glad you excused yourself." He said.

That night was just like any regular night. But This time around, Saleem didn't go back home; we stayed together in my apartment. Saleem later knelt and thanked my mum, which made her so emotional.

"Hallittah, with a mother's compassion, I wish you and Saleem all the best. May God guide and protect you," she said.

"Amen," I replied.

I looked at her. "Are you trying to run back to Gombe and leave me?"

She smiled. "Not yet."

The next day, Saleem and I went to check out his house. He carried me inside and dropped me on the couch, then went back to get my wheelchair. His room was upstairs, but he moved, arrangements were made for everything to be accessible downstairs for me.

He carried me to the room and sat me on the bed. My head rested on his shoulders. If someone were in the room, I believe they would have been able to hear our heartbeats.

He carried me and laid me on the bed. For the first time, we kissed. There was nothing as electrifying and impactful as that moment. He held me, and I laid on his chest.

"I have waited so long to have this moment with you," he said.

I lay on his chest and slept quietly. We woke up and went back to my apartment to eat because my mum always had food ready.

"I thought you weren't coming back," she teased.

"We came back for the food," I said.

Even though married, I always spent the night in my apartment, and Saleem went back to his. We agreed I would move to his house when we returned from Turkey.

Saleem made the arrangements for Turkey. My mum was to travel back to Gombe that same day we traveled out. Saleem arranged for a car to pick her from my apartment to Gombe.

My mum left very early in the morning. We said our goodbyes with tears in our eyes.

I was so excited for Turkey. We flew from Abuja to Istanbul. Saleem pushed my wheelchair; he wouldn't even allow anyone else to touch me. He put me on my seat, removed my backpack carrying every emergency aid I needed. We flew first class, our seats opposite each other. He was wide awake while I slept. Every time I woke up, he would turn to look at me.

We arrived in Istanbul and took a three-hour flight to Konya. That evening, when we arrived and checked in, we went straight to the Mevlana Museum, where Rumi's tomb is. It was very accessible with my wheelchair. The place was beautiful. There were other tombs, but Rumi's was the biggest. Next to it were writings in Persian, Rumi original manuscripts. I stood there, fascinated. My hands shook as I got close to the enclosed books.

I knew Saleem had not slept throughout the flight. I was also tired, so I suggested we go back to the hotel and return the next day. This would be the first time Saleem and I would be sleeping together in the same room. I was a bit shy because I needed to shower, but there was no support chair in the rest room even though Saleem had requested one before we came. The hotel apologized and said it would be brought. I decided I wouldn't shower, even though I really wanted to.

"I will close my eyes and bathe you." He said teasingly

I didn't want him to see the stitches and incisions the accident had left, but he gently persuaded me. He brought a towel, helped me pull off my clothes, and covered me. He went into the bathroom and regulated the water to a warm temperature. He carried me, holding me tight. I reached for the soap and washed as much as I could. The water drenched him, but he held me patiently. It was chaotic, but the sacrifice was enough. I rinsed off.

He brought me out, and I took a towel from the bathroom hanger. He wheeled me close to the bed. It felt awkward, but I managed. I was struggling to wear my pyjamas when he came out, he helped me and carried me to the bed. He showered, wore his pyjamas, laid beside me, and pulled me close, me against his chest.

The next day, our room was changed to one with a bathtub for easier bathing. I took my time washing and scrubbing. Saleem joined me inside the tub, I laid my back on him skin-to-skin, he caressed my hair and kissed my neck. He rinsed my body and carried me to the edge of the tub, cleaned my body with a towel, and took me to bed. We slept naked. The following day, we toured Konya and bought so many books. In the evening, we travelled back to Istanbul and then continued on to Verona, Italy.

We stayed indoors, reading, stealing glances, cuddling, and enjoying the view from our hotel balcony.

I could see Saleem's body respond to mine when we got close, but he never crossed his boundaries. He knew about my pelvic fracture from the accident and the spinal cord injury, which caused severe nerve damage and pain. The doctor said penetration might be impossible. But I still wanted to satisfy Saleem's intimate needs.

I wheeled my chair to where he was seated. "Are you okay?" he asked.

"Don't say anything," I whispered.

He gasped as I eased him. I left him perplexed while I shyly wheeled to the restroom to wash my hands and face. Later, he carried me to the bed and kissed me. He held me through the night.

We bonded intimately on this trip. When we got back home, I moved into his house.

Saleem's dad bought me the most sophisticated electronic wheelchair, with so many features, and had it shipped to me. I went to his house to thank him.

Hajiya made so much food, and we brought it home.

I gained more strength from therapy. I couldn't walk yet, but I could stand with my back brace. I spent most of my time indoors writing. Saleem was curious about what I had been writing.

"I am dying to read it," he said. "You never showed me what you wrote. I won't show you mine." I replied.

CHAPTER **21**

One evening, Saleem went out to get a paintbrush Hallittah had requested so she could start learning to paint. Hallittah took some bottles of cold water from the fridge, the wheelchair baba got her could increase in height allowing her to navigate around the house easily she poured them into a glass bowl to dip her face into it was one of her many beauty rituals. The glass fell and broke. She tried to manoeuvre her chair but got cut by the shards. She called Saleem, who rushed home. On seeing her, he insisted on taking her to the hospital, even though it was a minor cut. He was so worried that the nurses teased him for loving Hallittah so much that he couldn't even administer first aid.

The following morning, Saleem was so worried. He had a meeting with Baba but didn't want to leave Hallittah home alone.

"I'm going to be fine. Just go. I'll work around with my phone and call you when I need you," she reassured him. Zainab suggested borrowing her maid temporarily until they got a permanent one, after Saleem told her about Hallittah's accident.

When Saleem left for work, Hallittah helped herself to the shower. She slipped and fell hard on the bathroom floor, hitting her head and fracturing her backbone. The impact was so severe that she passed out. Saleem called around noon but got no answer. He called again, when got no reply. Panicking, he drove home.

When he didn't see her in the living room, he rushed into the bedroom and headed straight to the bathroom. She was lying unconscious. He covered her with a towel, carried her, dropped her in the car, and rushed to the hospital. "Please handle her with care," he told the doctors. She already has a spinal cord injury.

When Baba couldn't reach him, he called Zainab to go check in on Saleem as he has been unreachable. When Zainab drove to Saleem's, she walked in and called Baba: "Their phones are here, Hallittah's wheelchair is here." Baba alerted people to check every hospital. Meanwhile, Saleem was found, looking like a lost dog, seated on the floor. Zainab rushed to him, panicking.

Baba held Saleem and put him on the chair.

The doctor explained that the violent jolt on her back had aggravated her original spinal injury, and the fall also caused traumatic brain injury. Hallittah's mum, upon hearing about her fall, she traveled the following morning, praying and hoping. When she arrived at the hospital, she met a distraught Saleem, who hadn't left Hallittah's side. He had used the hospital showers and slept beside her, day in and day out.

He looked up at Hallittah's mum. "I am sorry," he said.

She smiled. "It's not your fault. I gave birth to a strong-willed daughter who does not like to ask for help. She always feels she can do everything. I can swear on the love you have for her, please let me take over from here. Go home and get some proper rest. Be strong for her," Hallittah's mum insisted, he left the hospital sadly.

The following day, when Zainab came to visit, Hallittah's mum begged her to find a way to make Saleem sleep. She feared for his health; lack of sleep might make him sick. Zainab told Baba about Saleem's situation. Hajiya made a meal and brought it to Saleem.

The drink was infused with a prescribed sleeping agent. Hajiya and Zainab spent the day at Saleem's house. By the time he woke up, it was very late at night. He woke up pissed that he overslept, excused himself, and drove to the hospital to see Hallittah.

Days turned into weeks. Saleem touched her face and whispered, "Please come back to me." Hallittah's mum sat in the corner with her huge Bible, praying softly. Then,

Hallittah opened her eyes. The doctors were called. Tears flowed from her eyes when she saw her mum and Saleem. The doctor advised her to remain still and avoid exertion.

Hallittah's mum kept saying, "thank you Jesus," while Saleem caressed her hair.

"You are the absolute love of my life, I am so sorry," she said.

To her mum, she said, "You are the strongest woman in the world, I love you, Mum." Her mum held her feet and wept.

Saleem refused to go home that day. He stayed beside her. The following morning, Hallittah touched his face. "You know, my grandpa was given the name 'Khasati' by his crush, Naima the girl he named me after. I once asked him what it meant. He had no clue, but he said to him it was the purest form of love." "Saleem, you are my Khasati," A tear dropped from his cheek, as she wiped it.

Hallittah looked at Saleem and asked, "tell me something", "I love you he said."

"Tell me something else, I know that already," she smiled. Do you know the smell of the earth you loved when the rain falls back at home, in Gombe that is called petrichor."

"I never knew that" she said, She smiled and closed her eyes to sleep. Hallittah never woke up. The alarms went off; the doctors rushed in and did everything they could, but she was gone. Saleem passed out. Hallittah's mum held her feet and cried.

"I will see you again. I will see you someday, somewhere where there is no hurt," she kept talking as though Hallittah could still hear her.

Saleem was resuscitated. He refused to spend a minute in bed or leave Hallittah's mum, who asked for some time alone with her daughter's body. He knelt beside Hallittah, kissing her hands, and held her mother up. Baba sent a driver to pick Saleem and Hallittah's mum and took them to the house. Hajiya was waiting, outside Saleem's house alongside with Baba and Aunty Dinatu. She took Hallittah's mother to the guest room.

Zainab, upon hearing the news, was inconsolable. Her husband Najeeb took her home.

When Chiamaka heard the news of Hallittah's death, she left her office. She fought through the Lagos traffic, urging her ride to drive fast, she bought a ticket at the airport, and boarded the available flight to Abuja. Upon arriving at Saleem's home, she found Hallittah's mother and held her as they wept.

Even though the law prohibited burials in residential areas, Saleem buried Hallittah on one of the lands he bought on the outskirts of Abuja, in the Gwagwalada region a potential site for the farmhouse Hallittah had always dreamed of.

Hallittah was buried according to Christian rites, assisted by Chisom's parents. Family and friends traveled to Abuja for the funeral. Saleem withdrew to his room upstairs and spoke little to anyone. After a month, Hallittah's mum went back home to Gombe.

Before leaving, she went upstairs with a bottle of kunun Zaki. "I have gained a son through this union. You have a beautiful heart. I never imagined a daughter of mine would marry a Muslim. It was against my beliefs, but you showed a love I never knew men were capable of. Hallittah loved her father deeply, and she always said she wanted a man like him. You are a great man. Do not let her death weigh you down. Mourn, but move on. Take care of yourself, or you will break my heart even more." She dropped the bottle and left.

That evening, Saleem visited his parents, then Zainab. He shared his plans to turn the land where Hallittah was buried into a garden. He invested in acquiring more land around the area and fenced it. He spent days on the land, which gradually became a beautiful garden. When he wasn't there, he stayed indoors writing. He hated visitors and only tolerated Zainab's presence at home.

After several months, he walked into the room he shared with Hallittah, brought out her journals, and read everything she wrote, it was their love story. That was when the name Khasati rang a bell. Hallittah had written in her journals *"Khasati is the purest form of love, a love that is innocently giving, just because"*. And she stopped there.

Saleem began to slip into depression, he spent days reading Hallittah's journal.

Zainab came to his house, crying, begging him to come out of it. she went upstairs to clean his room and saw the notes he had written, on reading them , she packed his work, and spent days arranging them, it was too deep , a body of work she has never seen before , his emotions where well-articulated, his hurt well written , she knew Saleem might not want to do anything about what he wrote looking at how scattered they were in his room, she sent it to her colleagues in the USA, who published it. When asked the title, she said, we would call it "Through *the Eyes of pain*". It did not take long, his work became a sensation across America, published as a non-fiction book, soon, Zainab began to receive emails, and mails, they kept flooding in.

She couldn't hide her secret any longer.

She went to Saleem's and made some tea for him, hoping to have a conversation with him "Would you like to publish your writings someday?"

"Never"

"Hallittah begged to read some of my writings; I refused. I'll write and burn them, so if you're getting any smart ideas, kill them."

Unknowingly, to him his work had become a global sensation. She sighed and left, knowing she had messed up.

Soon she began receiving emails inviting him to speak at functions. Zainab kept track of the earnings from the book. When she could no longer keep it a secret, she went to his house and found him writing.

"You are going to have back pain if you keep slouching like that," she said. He smiled.

"You wrote something beautiful something the world has never seen come out of Northern Nigeria. Love gave you pain, but it also gave you a voice. You will forgive me, because I did something you might not forgive. I took some of your work and published it. It has become a global bestseller. So many people have written emails to you. You are getting invitations to speak. Please forgive me."

He looked at her coldly and said nothing. She walked away crying.

A week later, Saleem went to Zainab's house and asked to see the emails. She showed him the reports, mails sent, publications, and record of the earnings.

"I forgive you," he said, and left.

The following day, Zainab came to see him and asked him what to do next. He answered angrily, "Figure it out. You started it. I am traveling to visit Hallittah's mum in Gombe."

Zainab felt terrible, but was hopeful that he would stop being angry, she knows he isn't acting like himself.

He spent three days at Hallittah's home in Gombe, then returned to Abuja and instructed Zainab to help set up a structure for the NGO Hallittah had started and keep it running. Later, he called Zainab and told her to publish Hallittah's story, from her journals. When she asked the title, he said "we will call it *Khasati*" *"what does that mean"*, *she asked,*

*"The readers will go through it and find out"*

www.ingramcontent.com/pod-product-compliance
Lightning Source LLC
Chambersburg PA
CBHW031945240626
47153CB00003B/868